ULTIMATE CHALLENGE

BOOK 8

Other Books in the
Spirit of the Game Series

ULTIMATE CHALLENGE

BOOK 8

BY TODD HAFER

zonder**kidz**

The children's group of Zondervan

www.zonderkidz.com

Ultimate Challenge
Copyright © 2005 by Todd Hafer

Requests for information should be addressed to
Zonderkidz, 5300 Patterson Ave., Grand Rapids, Michigan 49530

Library of Congress Cataloging-in-Publication Data
Hafer, Todd.
 Ultimate challenge / by Todd Hafer.
 p. cm. – (The spirit of the game ; bk.8)
 Summary: During the summer before his sophomore year in high school,
Cody competes in a statewide multisport challenge, relying on his Christian
faith to guide him both on and off the playing field.
 ISBN-10: 0-310-70797-8 (softcover)
 ISBN-13: 978-0310-70797-4
 [1. Christian life—Fiction. 2. Sportsmanship—Fiction. 3. Conduct of life—
Fiction. 4. Sports—Fiction. 5. High schools—Fiction 6. Schools—Fiction.] I.
Title.
 PZ7.H11975Ult 2005
 [Fic]–dc22
                                    2005018334

Interior design: Susan Ambs
Cover design: Alan Close
Art direction: Laura Maitner–Mason
Photos:Synergy Photographic

Special thanks to Zeeland Schwinn, Zeeland, Michigan.

Printed in the United States of America

05 06 07 08 • 5 4 3 2 1

Contents

To the life and memory of Tim Hanson,
a true athlete, a true friend.

Foreword

love sports. I have always loved sports. I have competed in various sports at various levels, right through college. And today, even though my official competitive days are behind me, you can still find me on the golf course working on my game, or on a basketball court playing a game of pickup.

Sports have also helped me learn some of life's important lessons—lessons about humility, risk, dedication, teamwork, and friendship. Cody Martin, the central character in the Spirit of the Game series, learns these lessons, too—some of them the hard way. I think you'll enjoy following Cody in his athletic endeavors.

Like most of us, he doesn't win every game or every race. He's not the best athlete in his school, not by a long shot. But he does taste victory because, as you'll see, he comes to understand that life's greatest victories aren't reflected on a scoreboard. They are the times when you rely on a strength beyond your own—a spiritual strength—to carry you through. They are the times when you put the needs of someone else before your own. They are the times when sports becomes a way to celebrate the life God has given you.

So read on, and may you always possess the true Spirit of the Game.

—Toby McKeehan

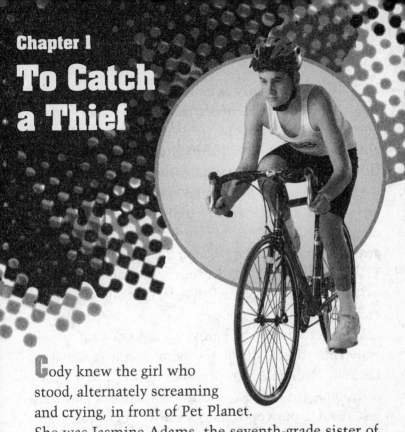

Chapter 1
To Catch a Thief

Cody knew the girl who stood, alternately screaming and crying, in front of Pet Planet. She was Jasmine Adams, the seventh-grade sister of Jessica Adams, one of the best athletes in the Grant High School freshman class.

Stealing a sevvy's purse? Cody thought, as he sprinted after the punk responsible for Jasmine's despair, *that is low. If I can get the purse back from this dude, I bet Jessica will give me a huge bear hug— for having her little sister's back. That might be kinda cool, but then again, it might make Robyn jealous. But maybe that wouldn't be such a bad thing.*

Cody smiled grimly as he saw the thief jump-stop, then dash down one of Cedar Heights Mall's long hallways. *Okay*, *Martin*, he scolded himself, *focus. Quit thinking about girl stuff and get your head into the game...except this is no game.*

He arrived at the hallway and paused for a moment. He studied a sign hanging from the corridor's low ceiling. RESTROOMS, read the sign's top line, with an arrow pointing left. The second line noted ADMINIS-TRATIVE OFFICES, with an arrow pointing right.

"No exit," Cody panted. "Dude, I got you now. You are so busted."

He jogged down the hallway. He veered right and tested the doorknob of the administrative offices. Locked. He smiled grimly and turned toward the restrooms. He walked past the ladies' room and was just about to push open the door to the men's facilities when a six-foot-tall, wide-eyed girl with a multi-wrapped ponytail burst from the ladies' room. "Dude!" she whispered, so loudly that she sounded like an angry cobra hissing, "there is, like, a guy in our bath-room. I'm sooooo gonna go tell security!"

Cody nodded. "Good idea," he said.

With that, the girl wheeled around and marched purposefully away, her yard-long ponytail swinging jauntily from side to side.

Cody waited until Ponytail Girl was out of sight before he cautiously pushed open the ladies' room door. *I doubt any other females are left in there,* he reasoned, *but I'm not taking any chances. I don't want anyone screaming at me or thinkin' I'm some kinda weirdo.*

He poked his head inside, scanning the room carefully. No one was in sight. He slid into the room. *Whoa,* he thought, crinkling his nose. *It smells pretty good in here, especially for a bathroom. It smells like pine trees or something. This is a whole other world from guys' bathrooms. And, check this out, they've even got a couch in here! Not sure why anyone would want to lounge around near a buncha toilets, but, still, it's kinda cool.*

He studied the four stalls to his right. The doors of the first three hung open. The last one was closed. He swallowed hard and positioned himself six feet in front of the door. In slow motion, he lowered himself into a baseball catcher's crouch. Then he tilted his head to the left, hoping to get a good low-angle view.

He saw two size-eleven sneakers pointing at him. *Okay,* he told himself, *there's no female with feet that huge, except for maybe Big Foot's wife. I've found my thief.* He stood and tilted his head toward the ceiling. *Father God,* he prayed, *please help me get that little sevvy's purse back—preferably without any bloodshed or broken bones, especially not mine. Amen.*

He stepped to the door. Using his right fist like a hammer, he pounded emphatically. Then he stopped and spoke, striving to make his fifteen-year-old voice sound like that of a thirty-something drill sergeant—a 250-pound drill sergeant. "Slide the purse under the door, man. Security's on the way, probably the police too. C'mon, dude. Give it up. You're caught."

Cody almost lurched back from the resulting wave of profanities that hit him.

Among the insults and threats of severe bodily harm, he heard a warning to flush all of Jasmine's purse contents down the toilet.

Well, he thought, smiling grimly. *I guess I'll take that as a no.* He studied the stall door, sizing it up like an opponent in football, calculating how much effort it would take to blast it open. *Kung fu kick or shoulder block?* he asked himself, taking two long steps backward.

In his mind, he heard a snap count, and he rushed the door, just as he had done playing wide receiver, exploding off the line of scrimmage to lay a fierce block on an opposing cornerback. He clenched his teeth and hurled his left shoulder into the door.

The door exploded inward. He felt it give under the force of his block then strike the thief. He wasn't sure about the point of impact—maybe the head, maybe the torso—but whatever the case, the thief was knocked backward, landing awkwardly on the toilet seat.

Cody studied the scene in front of him. The purse snatcher was sprawled across the commode seat, legs akimbo, eyes filled with terror and surprise, a pink Hello Kitty purse dangling from his right hand.

Where's a digital camera when you need one? Cody chuckled to himself.

The thief looked older, maybe sixteen or seventeen, but he appeared to be about Cody's size, maybe even smaller. Given his current position, it was hard to tell. One thing was obvious—the dude was stunned and scared.

"The purse," Cody commanded, holding out his hand.

The thief blinked a few times, then let the purse plop to the floor. Eyeing his opponent warily, Cody collected the purse and stepped back out of the stall. "Don't forget to flush," he said.

He almost collided with a stocky security guard as he exited the ladies' room. Jasmine and her friend trailed behind the guard.

"He's in there," Cody said to the guard, nodding toward the ladies' room door. "And," he added, turning to Jasmine and smiling, "I think this is yours."

"Thank you," Jasmine said, as if she'd just received an Academy Award.

"No problem," Cody shrugged. "Hey, you probably don't know me, but I know—"

"Oh, I *totally* know you, Cody Martin," Jasmine gushed, adjusting the straps of her plum-colored tank top. "Jess talks about you *a lot*. She says you're a stud."

Cody laughed sheepishly. "Oh," he said.

Jasmine looked at her friend, and they exchanged self-conscious giggles.

"Uh, if you don't mind," the security guard said, providing a welcome change of direction in the conversation, "I'm gonna need you girls to confirm that the subject in the lavatory is indeed the perpetrator."

Jasmine shook her head furiously. "Nuh-uh!" she proclaimed. "I don't want to have to see that dude ever again! What if he, like, attacks me or something?"

"It's okay, Jasmine," Cody assured. "I'll stand right by you. And this guard looks like he can handle himself too. We got your back."

The security guard smiled and nodded proudly. It looked to Cody like he was puffing out his chest to its maximum size.

"Here comes my backup," the guard said nodding toward the end of the hallway, where a taller, leaner security colleague appeared. "I will enter the restroom and apprehend the subject," he instructed. "You three wait here with Officer Lenny."

The stocky guard emerged a few moments later, his right hand clamped around the thief's elbow. "That's him!" Jasmine screeched. "That's totally him!"

"Yeah!" Jasmine's friend added, her head bobbing furiously, "that is *so* him! He's the thief!"

"Okay," Jasmine said, "I am getting creeped out now. My mom is picking us up at the main entrance, so, can we, like, go now?"

Officer Lenny nodded. "Yes," he said, "we have all we need from you. We'll take the subject to our holding area and wait for the police to arrive."

"How about I walk you to the entrance?" Cody offered.

"You are so sweet," Jasmine said emphatically. "Thank you!"

"Let's go, then," Cody said, leading the girls down the hallway. "I'm sure your mom will be eager to see you."

"Sir," the stockier guard called after Cody. "You need to make a statement, sir."

Cody wheeled around. "I'll come back and find you," he said. "But I need to take care of these girls first."

"Besides," he said, leveling his eyes at the purse snatcher, "I kinda already made my statement— Don't try to pull any garbage when there's a Grant High School varsity athlete around."

Chapter 2
Up to the Challenge?

"Your turn," Pork Chop Porter said to Cody, pointing to the lat-pull machine.

Cody positioned himself in the seat in front of the lat-pull bar, a long, horizontal metal cylinder, bent down at a 45-degree angle at both ends. He grabbed the handgrips and pulled. The stack of weights barely budged. He felt a sharp, pinching pain between his neck and left shoulder. "Uh, Chop," he said, "you wanna move the pin to a weight that I can actually move? What—you got like two hundred pounds on there or something?"

Chop chuckled. "Close. Sorry, dawg; I forgot to take the man-weights off after I finished my set. Or maybe I wanted to test how swole you're gettin'. After all, we've been working out like crazy ever since school got out."

"I am getting stronger," Cody said. "But I still weigh under a buck fifty, and if you've got 190 or something loaded on the machine, it isn't going anywhere. I mean, c'mon. Do the math, big dawg."

To emphasize his point, Cody tightened his grip on the lat-pull bar, then did a chin-up, letting his legs dangle above the seat. "See what I mean?" he grunted, before lowering himself back to the seat. "You can't fight physics."

Chop shook his head. "Dawg, you gotta get more junk in your trunk. You wanna lay some serious hits on wide receivers come football season? You need at least fifteen more pounds of muscle."

Cody nodded. "Maybe. But I gotta make sure I can still get my speed on. I can't get too big."

"Speed?" Chop countered. "You got decent wheels— I'll give you that. But you're not exactly Craig Ward. Not even Terry Alston."

"Well, Chop, which one of us has a state track silver medal?"

Pork Chop let out a bark of laughter. "Touché," he said. "I gotta admit—that was fierce. You did hold it down on the ol' two-mile relay. You ran a flat out guts race."

Chop adjusted the weight to 115 pounds. "One more set, Code," he said. "And we're done for today. Finish strong, 'cuz I got a little present for ya when we're done."

Cody sat at his kitchen table, studying the "present" Chop had given him after their preseason workout at the Grant High gym was complete—a brochure for a competition billed as "The Search for Colorado's Ultimate Teen Athlete."

"Yeah, right," he muttered. "Cody Martin, the Ultimate Athlete. I can't believe Chop thinks I would even have a prayer in something like this."

He continued to read, growing less optimistic with each nugget of new information about the competition. Ten events over two days, testing the athletes' strength, speed, endurance, skills, and mental toughness. Sprinting, distance running, a twenty-mile bike race. Bench pressing your body weight. One-on-one basketball. "And look at this," he said. "The shot put. Too bad Chop's hand is still weak from his brawl with Alston this past spring. He'd win that event for sure."

Cody startled when Beth entered the room. "Hey, Code," she said cheerfully, "you praying—or just talking to yourself again?"

He felt a strange knot forming in his stomach, the same one that first appeared seven months ago, when Beth became the second wife of Luke Martin and officially moved into the family home. "Uh, sorry, Beth," he said. "I was just reading about this competition that Chop wants me to do, and it's such a ridiculous idea that I guess it got me muttering to myself."

Beth frowned. "What makes it so ridiculous, Cody? You're a good athlete."

"You're just saying that because you're ... uh, married to my dad."

Cody saw Beth's lips draw tight. *I think she's mad that I didn't call her my mom—or even stepmom,* Cody reasoned. *I hate to see that frustrated look on her face—I truly don't want to upset her, but, man, she's not my mom. Cancer got the only mom I'll ever have, and that's that.*

"Cody," Beth said, interrupting his thoughts, "I think you should compete. Look, you decided not to play baseball this summer; you're gonna need something to help you keep your edge. Besides, remember what Ecclesiastes says?"

Cody shrugged. "Not the whole book of Ecclesiastes. You wanna be more specific?"

Beth walked toward him and swatted him playfully across the top of the head. "Specific, eh, wise guy?

Well, how about this—'The race is not to the swift, or the battle to the strong.' That's chapter nine, verse eleven. In case you didn't know."

Cody scratched his head. "That's in Ecclesiastes, huh? I thought it was in Proverbs."

Beth smiled. "You can look it up if you want. But I'm right. More important, the verse is right. I've seen some posters for the competition around town. It's ten events, and you score points for how you do in each one. It favors a multisport jock like you. It's kinda like the Olympic decathlon."

Cody snorted. "I know. And I'm no decathlete. Those guys are studs! Me, I'm just a role player. I do the dirty work. I do the little things. Don't get me wrong—I don't resent that role at all. Coach Clayton tells me all the time, 'Every good team needs a junk-yard dawg like Cody Martin.' That makes me feel good. But I don't see how a role player like me belongs in a competition for elite athletes. I'll leave that to Alston, Craig Ward, Brendan Clark. You know, the hosses. I know Chop would enter, if his hand was completely healed—and if he wasn't so bummed about moving away next month."

Cody studied Beth, waiting for a rebuttal. She stood, tapping her forefinger on her lower lip. "Tell you what," she said finally. "You enter this competition.

You train hard. And at Christmas break, I will fly you to Tennessee so you can spend a week or so with Mr. Porter. Deal?"

Cody ejected from his chair. "Are you serious! That would be so cool!"

"I'm as serious as an algebra test. And, I'll go you one better. You place in the top three in your age group, and I'll let you help me name the baby." She rubbed her stomach for emphasis.

Cody smiled. It looked like Beth was smuggling a volleyball inside her shirt. Soon, it would be a basketball, and eventually, perhaps, a medicine ball. "What makes you think I want to help name the baby?" he asked.

"Well, don't you?"

"Hmmm. Now that you mention it, it would be kind of cool. But what about Dad—doesn't he want a vote?"

Beth laughed dismissively. "You want to know what Mr. Luke Martin wants to name this poor innocent child? Milo, if it's a boy. Destaline if it's a girl. He says he's never heard of a girl with such a unique name."

Cody widened his eyes. "Well," he said, "there's a good reason for that. *Destaline?* That sounds like some kind of industrial solvent. And Milo? Milo Martin? That poor kid would get razzed right outta elementary school."

Beth nodded. "Precisely. So, you can see why I'm kicking your dad off the naming committee. It's all on you and me, dude." With that, she opened a drawer and handed Cody a pen. "Better get to filling out the entry form. When you're done, give it to me, and I'll mail it for you. Then you better get outside and start training."

"But Chop and I already lifted today, over at the school."

"You do any cardio?"

Cody bowed his head. "Well, uh, no."

Beth clapped her hands together. "Well, there you go, then. Call Drew Phelps and go for a run. Or call Robyn and run with her, if you'd prefer."

Cody stroked his chin dramatically. "Let's see," he said. "Drew would really push me. He says he is going to try to put in a thousand miles this summer. And, of course, there's also the fact that he's an insane running machine. Named all-state as a freshman. But, on the other hand, Robyn is way better lookin'. And she smells better too."

Beth plucked the kitchen phone from its charger. "Robyn Hart it is, then, I guess," she said. "Just don't start making googly eyes at her and step in a pothole and bust your ankle!"

Cody returned from his four-mile run with Robyn and searched in vain for some kind of sports drink in the refrigerator. Four miles wasn't a killer run, but the temperature was in the mid-80s—unexpectedly hot for a Colorado early-July day.

Robyn had been unusually quiet, and Cody hoped it was the heat, not something else that suppressed the conversation. He stood for a while in front of the refrigerator, letting some of its coolness drift over him. He spied a can of one of Beth's meal-replacement shakes on the top shelf. *I wonder how this stuff tastes*, he thought. He studied the label. *Chocolate flavored—so that's a good thing. And it's cold.* He shook the can vigorously, then pulled the metal tab on the top.

Cody dashed to the sink and spewed out the beverage like a geyser. "Nas-tee!" he said. "Ugh, how does Beth stomach this stuff?"

The phone rang. He looked at the caller ID.

"Hey, Chop," he said, "give me a second, will ya?"

He set the phone down, filled a glass with water, then used it to gargle away every remnant of the vile protein shake.

He heard Pork Chop chuckling when he returned to the phone. "What happened, dawg? You chug some milk that was on its way to becoming cottage cheese?"

"Worse, Chop. You know, Beth drinks these high-protein, low-carb shakes in a can. So, I get back from running with Robyn, and I need something to drink, right? So I try one of these things. The label says it's chocolate, but it tastes like a bunch of chemicals, kinda metallic or something. It was just nasty."

"Well, dawg, you really don't drink protein shakes for the taste; you drink 'em for the protein."

"Yeah, but dude! How does a person stomach this crud? It was, like, all thick too. Like the stuff Mom used to give me when I had diarrhea!"

Chop was laughing again. "You done now? That all you got for me? 'Cuz I need to bust your chops a little. But I can wait if you want to continue your critique of the girl-shake."

"Sorry, Chop. I didn't mean to go on and on. I'm just still amazed that people actually pay money for this stuff. But—hey, what are you gonna bust on me for? I can't remember doing anything stupid, at least not in the past couple of weeks."

"You got it all wrong, Code. You did something *right*. Really right. Righteous, in fact. The only thing you did wrong was not tell me about it."

Cody thought for a moment. "Uhh—"

"C'mon now, little brother. You're playin' with me. Last week—at Cedar Heights Mall? That ring a bell at all?"

Cody cleared his throat nervously. "Oh yeah. That. That was pretty fierce, but how am I gonna bring up something like that without sounding like I'm bragging? And you know how I feel about inflatin' my own tires."

"I'm sorry, dawg, but you play Super Action Hero like that, chase a dude through the mall, bust down a bathroom door, and retrieve a little sevvy's purse … you do something like that, and you've got a right to beat your chest a little."

Cody felt himself smiling. "Well, it *was* pretty intense. I kinda thought somebody would tell you about it, then we could talk. You know. See, there's this Proverb that says, 'Let another praise you, and not your own mouth; someone else, and not your own lips.'"

Cody heard Pork Chop groan on the other end of the line. "Man, that's the thing with you church boys—you got a verse for every situation, don't you?"

"Isn't that the point?"

A few seconds passed before Chop spoke again. "Well, let me ask you this, then. What verse was it that drove you to chase down a nineteen-year-old dude with a juvy record and lay the smackdown on him, huh?"

"That's a fair question, Chop. But the Bible says that love always protects; you know that. We learned that back when you used to go to Sunday school with me every week—back in the day. Remember those times? Anyway, then, there's this other verse. It's in James, I think, and it says something like, 'He who knows the good he should do and doesn't do it, sins.' See, I couldn't just stand by and let that dude rip Jasmine off like that. Traumatize her, you know? Then, there's the whole concept of the Old Testament judges. Check this out, back in the day—"

"Okay, okay, okay." Chop's voice was weary. "You made your point. And don't get me wrong—what you did was totally bomb. It's just hard to figure sometimes. I mean, I remember the story of how Jesus tore it up when he cleared the temple. I remember that Pastor Taylor said that those tables he was tossing around weighed a coupla hundred pounds. But, then, isn't Jesus also supposed to be the Prince of Peace?"

Cody uttered a quick prayer for wisdom before he spoke. "Look at it this way, Chop. Do you think Jasmine is at peace right now—and would she have been if that punk had gotten away with all her money, student ID, and who knows whatever personal girl-stuff was in her purse? And how peaceful a place would Cedar Heights Mall be if a bunch of wannabe gangstas thought they could steal, harass, vandalize, whatever—and get away with it? Peace is a big concept, Chop. There's more to it than just not fighting.

Don't get me wrong. I've been second-guessing myself ever since it all went down. Maybe I shoulda just waited for a security guard to show up. I just wanted to bust in and get the purse before it was too late."

"Yeah, I'm kinda feelin' that, Code. It's just hard, trying to understand what God wants you to do in every situation, trying to figure out what all the verses mean."

"It is hard, Chop. I never said it wasn't hard; I just said it was true. You want an easy religion . . . go worship a tree or something."

Cody waited for his friend's good-natured laughter to subside before posing the question that had been needling him for the past five minutes. "Hey, Chop, you said that purse-grabber was nineteen? For real?"

"For reals, little brother. His name's Fulton, and he's full-on one-niner. Four years older than you and me. You took down a grown-up, dawg! You're diesel!"

Cody whistled through his teeth. "Whoa! Nineteen, huh? I'm sooo glad I prayed before I went after him. But you know—he looked a lot younger than nineteen sitting there on the toilet, holding a purse."

Two weeks after Beth mailed in Cody's Ultimate Athlete entry, a large tan envelope arrived at the Martin household. Cody eagerly tore open the top of the envelope and dumped its contents on the kitchen table. The competition was August 15, just four weeks away. And there was an informational meeting in Denver in less than a week.

Cody sat at the table and began to read through all the rules, event descriptions, and the scoring system. His head was reeling by the time his dad and Beth entered the house with a large bag of Chinese take-out food.

"I'm really proud of you for entering this competition, son," Cody's dad said, waving a half-eaten egg roll for emphasis. "You're challenging yourself, stepping out of your comfort zone. That will stretch you as a person."

"I'm afraid it might tear me right in half," Cody groaned. "It'll be like being put on the rack—that's how far it will stretch me. It says here that the best athletes in the whole state will compete. Aw, I must be crazy."

Beth used a chopstick to slide a glossy piece of paper across the table toward her. "It says here," she said slowly, reading as she spoke, "that there's a fifteen-and-under division. Last time I checked, you're fifteen. So you'll be competing only against guys your age—and younger."

Cody felt his head wagging vigorously from side to side. "Yeah, but do you know who else is fifteen?

Cabrera, Clay, Locke, Jones, Miller, Mack, Nakamura. I think Macy turns sixteen this month, around the same time Alston does, so maybe he's off the table. But still. Those other guys are animals—and they're just the ones I know of. I can only imagine what kinda hosses are going to come over from the other side of the state—Grand Junction, Aspen, Durango. Oh, and I almost forgot the other Grant High guys. Terrance Dylan's competing. So is Marcus Berringer. The Evans twins are way into baseball, thank goodness, but to top it all off, Drew Phelps doesn't turn sixteen till the day after the competition. So he's gonna be there. And he's so intense a competitor that it's downright scary."

Beth frowned. "Drew's a great runner, Cody," she said. "But he's so skinny. I bet he can barely pick up a shot put, let alone toss it anywhere. And I bet he has trouble bench pressing his covers off his chest when he wakes up in the morning."

Cody shook his head dismissively. "Don't let his size fool you. Sure, he weighs only a buck thirty, but he's wiry. He's all lean muscle. He's stronger than you think. Just ask Goddard. I think he still has a welt on his stomach where Phelps drilled him with a dodge ball the last week of school. And besides, do you have any idea how many points he's gonna rack up in the 5K? And the twenty-mile bike ride? That's like a warm-up for him!"

Beth smiled. "What about basketball?"

Cody grinned. "He's got the touch of a gorilla. I'll kill him in basketball."

"Ah," she said. "At last, a touch of confidence from Cody Martin. And a sense of humor to boot. That's how to approach it, Code. Work from your strengths. Have fun. Learn something about yourself maybe."

"Like what? That I'm so NOT the Ultimate Athlete?"

Beth was about to speak, but Cody's dad held up his palm. "If I may," he said to her.

Beth shrugged. "Hey, he's got your DNA. He's all yours, babe. Just pass me the soy sauce, and I'll shut up."

Cody's dad plopped his elbows on the table and steepled his twiggy fingers. "The people who organized this competition," he said, "probably think the person who wins the most events, scores the most points, is the Ultimate Athlete. But, I challenge you, son, to think bigger than that. Maybe the Ultimate Athlete isn't the guy who's the strongest or fastest. What about being the Ultimate Sportsman, the Ultimate Competitor, the Ultimate Role Model for all the young kids who will be watching?"

"Okay," Beth said, her mouth still half-full of kung pao chicken, "*that* is good advice. That was way-better than what I was gonna say. You da man, Luke!"

Cody saw his father's face flush. "I suppose I am," he said quietly. "It's not inconceivable that I'm da man."

Chapter 3
The Emergency Room

Cody sat in the back row of Denver Northwest High School's auditorium, flanked by Drew Phelps on his left and Marcus Berringer and Terrance Dylan on his right. He watched the athletes milling around in front of them. Many wore sleeveless T-shirts and throwback basketball jerseys that showcased their thickly muscled, tattooed arms.

Cody leaned to Drew. "Okay, if these guys are all fifteen and under, I'm the king of France."

Drew replied with something about "the maturation process," but Cody wasn't listening. He saw East High's Bobby Cabrera enter the auditorium.

I just knew he'd *be here,* Cody thought sullenly as he eyed his longtime foe. *I was hoping I could go the whole summer without him getting in my face, but that's doubtful now. Aw, I'm getting sick to my stomach. I should get outta here and see if there's something better going on in another room. A summer yoga class, Future Farmers of America meeting, a bell-choir rehearsal, anything!*

An arena-league football player Cody had never heard of kicked off the meeting, punctuating each point he made by slamming a grapefruit-sized fist into his palm. He used the word "intense" at least once a sentence. He finished by screaming hoarsely, "In just one month, we'll all be back here to find out who is, truly, the Ultimate Athlete. So don't bring your name; bring your game!"

The speech elicited a few whoops from the audience, only half of which seemed sincere to Cody.

A statuesque woman with coal black hair claimed the stage next. She was introduced as a top fashion model and former dancer for the Denver Nuggets. *This time*, Cody observed, *the whoops and whistles are all sincere.*

"I'm here to explain the rules of the competition," Ms. Top Model said cheerfully. "So I need everyone's attention."

"I don't think she even needed to ask for that," Drew whispered sarcastically.

Cody nodded. *She is impressive*, he thought. *And she's gotta be, like six feet, two inches. But, still, she's no Robyn Hart.*

After the rules overview and a few concluding comments from one of the event organizers, the athletes began to file out of the auditorium. Cody noted that many of the competitors were clustered around Ms. Former Nugget Dancer, like honeybees around their queen.

The arena-league baller, conversely, attracted only a handful of autograph seekers. "Dude," observed Berringer, "I've been in huddles with more guys than that. But if I want to meet the model, I'll have to wait for an hour, at least."

"We don't have that kinda time," Cody said, glancing at his watch. "Terrance's dad is gonna pick us up in front of the school in about five minutes."

As Cody and his teammates glided toward the exit, he swiveled his head around, trying to spot Cabrera. He didn't see his archrival, but he did notice Locke, a stallion from Lincoln High, headed his way. *It figures he'd be here too*, Cody thought. *Man, he's getting tall. He must be six feet, one inch now, if not more. He's got a couple inches on me; that's for sure. That'll be trouble come basketball season.*

"Hey, Martin, Dylan," Locke called. "I wondered if I'd see you guys here."

"Hey, Locke," Terrance greeted, extending his right hand.

"Yeah, hey," Cody added. "What's up?"

Cody saw Locke studying Berringer. "Do I know you?" he asked finally. "You look kinda familiar."

To Cody's ear, Berringer's voice sounded more nasal and sarcastic than usual. "Well, if you woulda played varsity football this past season, you woulda seen a lot of me. I played offense and defense. But you played just frosh and JV ball, didn't you, Locke? Didn't see any varsity action."

Locke shrugged. "Lincoln's a bigger school than Grant. We aren't hurting for athletes the way the little farm towns are. It's not like you can just show up with a pulse and make a team."

Berringer narrowed his eyes and took a step toward Locke. "Dude, I hope you play some varsity wide receiver this year. 'Cuz I'll jack you up! Our defensive backfield is called the No Passing Zone, and you're gonna find out why!"

Cody saw Locke's hands curl into fists. He quickly stepped in front of Berringer. "Okay," he said, struggling to keep his voice from quivering. "Let's chill, all right? Hey, Locke, where's Madison? I thought he would be here."

Locke wagged his head. "Nah, he's thinking about it, but he's on two different baseball teams right now.

And, man, he's throwing fire this summer."

"Yeah," Drew interjected. "I hear he's got college scouts interested in him already."

"Well," Locke responded, "I do see a lot of guys with clipboards at his games."

"That's cool," Cody said, a bit too enthusiastically. "If you see him, tell him good luck this summer. I'm glad I won't be facing him. I don't wanna get plunked by another one of his fastballs! Anyway, we gotta go."

Cody grabbed Berringer's wrist and tugged firmly. "Wait!" Berringer hissed. "I'm not done with him yet."

"You're done," Dylan said flatly. "Unless you wanna walk home."

Cody had his hand on the back door of Mr. Dylan's Montero when he heard the voice behind him. "Martin, wait up!"

Cody turned and faced Cabrera, sporting his trademark sneer. "Mr. Cabrera," he said, trying to sound casual—and unintimidated.

"I wondered if you'd be here," Cabrera said, smoothing the front of his East High football T-shirt. "I wondered if you'd give this competition a go."

"I knew you'd be here," Cody said. "This should be a good competition for a multisport athlete like you."

Cabrera cocked his head and eyed Cody suspiciously. "Yeah? Well, you know, you're right. In fact, I plan to win." He paused, looking for a moment at Dylan, Drew, and Berringer. The rest of you? You're all just going for second place."

Cody expected Berringer to jump all over that line, but his fellow defensive back just stood sullenly, arms folded across his chest.

Hmm, Cody pondered. *Cabrera is shorter than Locke by a good three inches—and it looks like he's gotta be fifteen pounds lighter too. He can't weigh more than a buck forty-five. And Berringer's at least a 160-pounder. And yet I can tell he's intimidated.*

"What?!" Cabrera said, finally breaking the tense silence. "You all got nothing for me? Or do you just know what I said is true—and you're scared?"

Berringer studied his shoes.

Mr. Dylan started to exit from his SUV, but Terrance waved him back in. Then he locked eyes with Cabrera and spoke in a voice that was eerily low and calm. "I'll let what I do in the competition speak for me," he said.

"We'll see," Cabrera said.

"Yes," Terrance said, "we will. But there is one thing I need to say. I'm not afraid of you. If you didn't know that, now you know."

Cabrera opened his mouth and started to speak. But, after studying Terrance's face for a moment, he closed his mouth and smiled. "Like I said, we'll see. But I know I'm gonna smoke all of you. Especially you, Martin! You don't even belong in a competition like this."

Cody shrugged. "I think you said it best, 'We'll see,'" he answered. "Good luck, though, Cabrera. Really. I do think you have a good chance of winning."

Cabrera turned and swaggered away, shaking his head in apparent disbelief.

Cody saw the hastily scrawled note as soon as he entered the living room. It was hard to miss taped in the center of the television screen. The message was simple:

> *AT THE HOSPITAL.*
> *TROUBLE WITH THE BABY.*
> *WILL CALL SOON.*
> *PLEASE PRAY!*
> *LOVE, DAD & BETH*

Cody grabbed the phone and checked the messages. There was only one, from Blake Randall, Cody's youth pastor at Crossroads Community Church. "I just heard there might be complications with Beth's pregnancy," Blake's voice was calm yet concerned. "Please let me know what I can do."

Maybe I should jump on my bike and get over to Grant Hospital, Cody thought. *Or I could call Blake and ask him for a ride. But then again, I'm just assuming they went to the local hospital. Maybe they drove to the Springs. After all, that's where they plan to have the baby.*

Cody paced the living room, weighing his options. Should he start calling hospitals? Would they give him any information? Finally, he decided to call Pork Chop. The Porter farm, east of Grant, was a good fifteen minutes away by truck. But that might be the quickest option. It would take at least that long to bike to the local hospital—and then what would happen if that wasn't the right one? Blake was probably en route to the hospital, if not there already, and that's where Blake was needed. A call from Cody Martin would probably be a distraction.

"It's times like these," Cody whispered, "that I really wish Dad would let me have a cell phone. I could get on my bike and make calls while I was on the move."

The phone rang, and Cody instinctively dashed for the kitchen, where the phone charger was. He was halfway there when he realized the phone was still in his hand.

"Hello?" he said, hearing the anxiety in his own voice.

"Cody," Blake said, "I'm glad you're home."

"B, what's going on? Is Beth going to be okay? Is the baby—"

"I can't say right now, Code," came the reply. "Beth started hemorrhaging an hour or so ago. She was also having some strong contractions. Your dad got her to the hospital right away, so that's a very good thing."

Cody felt his mouth growing dry. "What does this mean, B? It's only mid-July; she's more than two months away from her due date."

"What it means is that the people here at Grant Hospital need to keep your little brother or sister right where it is. It's too early. Look, Pastor Taylor is here holding things down, so I'm coming to get you. Be ready. And pray hard."

"Okay," Cody said quietly.

He hung up the phone and closed his eyes. *Dear God*, he prayed, *I'm scared. My dad and Beth have been so happy. They must be terrified now. Please help Beth to stop bleeding. And please, please protect my little brother! Amen.*

I don't remember the last time Dad hugged me like this, Cody thought as his father wrapped his wiry arms around him.

Luke's voice was quivering as he spoke—"I'm so glad you're here, Cody. I don't know if I can handle having the woman I love in dire straits in a hospital again."

Cody could think of nothing to say, so he simply hugged his dad tightly.

Cody stood beside his father at a pay phone in the main lobby of Grant Hospital. "Yes," Luke was saying, "the bleeding has stopped, thank God. But then, at first, they had trouble finding the baby's heartbeat with that, uh, microphone thing they glide over Beth's stomach. But then they picked up the sound. Good and strong. Kind of fast too. But no faster than mine at the time . . . What's that? Yes, of course. Thank you, sir. You're a good man."

Cody's dad cradled the receiver and sighed heavily.

"Who was that, Dad?" Cody asked. "Your brother?"

"No. My boss. But I guess I should call Larry. We haven't spoken in a while. Uh, Cody?"

"Yeah, Dad?"

"Thank you for being here. Thank you for your prayers. The doctor said everything will be fine, but Beth is going to have to take it very easy from this point on. She might even have to go on strict bed rest. That will mean more responsibility for you."

Cody nodded approvingly. "No problem, Dad. You just tell me what needs to be done. I'll help you take care of Beth—and little you-know-who."

Cody could see relief wash over his father's face. "Thank you so much, son."

"I'm happy to do it, Dad. Besides, it's not like I have school to worry about, just training for this Ultimate Athlete thing, and I'm probably gonna get worked in that anyway."

Cody's dad rubbed his temples with his thumbs for a moment. "I appreciate your attitude, Cody, but there's also the fact that Deke Porter, your best friend in the whole world, is moving in just three weeks. I know you want to spend as much time as possible with him. I feel bad that—"

"Aw, don't worry about that, Dad. I'll just have Chop come over a lot. Put him to work. The both of us can fetch stuff for Beth and make sure the house is cleaned up. Let's just make sure the refrigerator is all stocked up."

Cody saw his dad smile, and he felt the knot that had formed in his stomach the moment he first heard the bad news finally relax, then disappear. The sensation that replaced it was warm, peaceful. He draped his right arm across his dad's shoulders, noticing that the two guys in the Martin household were now almost exactly the same height. "Hey, Dad," he said quietly, "let's go see Beth."

"Cody!" Beth said, half raising her torso from her emergency room bed the moment he peeked his head in. A grandmotherly nurse was unhooking a giant belt-like contraption from Beth's stomach. "Just let me get this hardware off your mom, young man," the nurse said, "and you can give her a big ol' bear hug!"

Cody smiled. In the past, he knew he would have corrected the nurse, with, "Uh, she's not really my mom." But not today. Beth's smile had widened when she heard the M-word, and Cody resolved to do nothing to dim that smile.

Man, Cody thought, as Beth pulled him to her a few moments later. *She hugs as hard as my dad. She's pretty strong, for a girl—especially one who's spent the afternoon in a hospital!*

"I'm so relieved for you," Cody said, when Beth finally released him from the power hug. "I was praying like crazy."

Beth's eyes were moist with concern. "You were really worried about your little sibling, weren't you, dude?"

Cody rested his right hand on Beth's shoulder. "I was worried about you, too."

Now Beth's eyes were more than moist. They were officially teary. She covered Cody's hand with one of her own. "That means so much to me," she sniffled. "I can't even tell you."

Cody nodded. "I was just praying that God would help you be okay," he said. "I didn't want anything bad to happen to you. I remember pleading, 'Please, please protect Beth. And please, please protect my little brother!'"

Cody saw Beth's mouth curl into a sly grin. "Cody," she said, cocking her head, "what you just said—were those your exact words?"

Cody thought for a moment. "Yeah. Pretty much. More than pretty much, in fact. I remember that prayer, because it was so intense. So desperate. Why?"

Beth's eyes were sparkling. "Do you realize what you just said?"

Cody frowned in concentration. "Uh . . . I guess I'm kinda lost here."

Beth poked him in the ribs. "What? It's summer break so you give your brain a couple of months off? Think about your prayer: 'Please protect my little—'"

Cody felt his mouth drop open. "Brother!" he shouted. "I said 'little brother'—that's right. But why would I say that? I don't know the baby's gender. Even you and Dad don't know. The only ones who know are God and your doctors. So, where did 'brother' come from? Maybe it was just a slip of the tongue."

"Maybe," Beth said, but the tone of her voice betrayed her. "But, then again—"

Cody could hear the excitement in his voice. "What are you thinking—or do you know something? C'mon, give me the scoop. I promise I won't tell Dad when he comes back in. A nurse or a doctor spilled the beans, huh?"

"I don't really know anything Cody. It's just that you prayed what you prayed, and when I was first lying here with my hands on my stomach, terrified, I remembered that I begged God, 'I don't care what happens to me, but please protect this little baby boy.' *Boy.* So, Cody Martin, either our boy-prayers are just some weird coincidence or it's a God thing."

Cody smiled as a memory flashed in his brain. "My mom didn't believe in coincidences," he said. "I know what she'd say about this."

Cody stepped back, fearing that what he'd just said would wound Beth's feelings. There was always that uneasy silence every time he mentioned his mom. But today, on Beth's face he saw only peace.

"Your mom was a smart woman," Beth said, smiling. "Let's go with her on this one."

"Well, it would be cool to have a little brother," Cody noted. "Somebody to protect and teach sports to. If I start working with him when he's really young, he could be one fierce athlete by the time he's old enough to compete."

"Teaching him sports would be nice. But what about reading? That's kinda important too, last time I checked."

Cody could feel the heat of his blushing cheeks. "Oh, yeah. Of course, reading. A little dude's gotta know how to read. How else is he gonna know how the Broncos are doing in the AFC West? And you gotta be able to read to understand baseball box scores. Those things can be kind of complicated. And there are some great sports biographies—"

Beth's laughter interrupted Cody in midsentence. "You are a true jock, aren't you, dude?"

Cody shrugged. "What can I say?"

"You can say, Cody Martin, that you'll read your little brother Bible stories first, *then* the sports stuff. Deal?"

Cody extended his hand to Beth. "Deal," he said.

Chapter 4

Good-byes and a Surprise

Cody rebounded Pork Chop's errant free throw and fired a chest pass to his friend, who had moved to the top of the key of the outdoor court behind Grant High School. Chop launched a jump shot that fell short by three feet. "Aw, dawg," he moaned, gazing sadly at his right hand, "all that time in a cast musta really ruined my touch. It's like I'm learning to shoot all over again."

Cody grinned. "With your shot, maybe that's not such a bad thing, big man."

"Ha, Ha, ha. Your attempts at humor, little brother, that's one thing I'm *not* gonna miss."

"If my material's so tired, then why are you smilin', huh?"

Chop snorted. "I'm just trying to keep from bruisin' your fragile ego."

"Whatever," Cody said, checking his watch. "Hey, man, it's almost time. We should head over to Louie's Pizza. The dinner in your honor is gonna be ready soon."

Chop banked in a shot from the low block. "You didn't have to organize this thing, you know. I don't need a big send-off."

Cody collected his ball and tucked it under his right arm. "You deserve it. Now let's go have some pizza—or whatever."

"Uh, what do you mean 'whatever,' dawg? Louie's doesn't really serve anything *but* pizza."

Cody winked at him. "You'll see," he said.

Louie's was more crowded than Cody had ever seen it—including when he and the Grant eighth graders upset Central at the Grant Hoops Invitational a year and a half ago. Mike Dawes, the owner, grumbled good-naturedly about fire-code violations as he placed extra chairs at the heads of all the booths along the pizza shop's perimeter.

Once the crowd was settled, Mike welcomed the throng to his restaurant, then introduced Coach

Clayton. The lanky basketball and track coach slid to the front of the restaurant amid barking cheers of "Coach! Coach! Coach!" from the Grant High School athletes, who made up 75 percent of those in attendance.

Once the noise subsided, Coach Clayton doffed his zebra-striped baseball cap and began his speech. "I've been around sports since I was a knot on a log," he said in his Tennessee drawl, "so I've seen a lot of athletes in my time. But, hand to God, I never met one quite like Pork Chop Porter. I mean, for the love of Charles Barkley, does the Chop move well for a big man! He's got skills."

"Amen, brother! Preach it!" Chop called out.

"Humility too," Coach Clayton countered quickly, drawing hoots from the crowd. "But, to be serious again for a while, Pork Chop is one coura-geous athlete. I've seen him play through pain, through exhaustion. I saw him start on the high school offensive line as a freshman this past season, going face mask to—face mask with some of the biggest, ugliest monsters in this part of the state. Especially Claxton Hills. All y'all know how ugly those country club boys are—of course their mommies and daddies are so rich that they can afford plastic surgery for 'em!"

Cody smiled as the laughter exploded all around him. Pork Chop was laughing so hard that for a moment Cody feared he might choke.

When he had retrieved the crowd's attention again, the coach concluded—"The only other thing I want to say is that Mr. Porter is one fine teammate. He makes the players around him better, and if somebody cheap-shots one of his homeys, he's gonna have to answer to the big man. Ain't that right, Cody Martin?"

Cody nodded emphatically, like a bobble-head doll on a paint-shaking machine.

"Anyway," Coach Clayton said, "I hope y'all have enjoyed watching Mr. Porter get his sports on these past few years, because we won't see the likes of him again. God bless ya, big Chop. And when you get down Tennessee way, have yourself a sweet tea and some barbecue for me, ya hear?"

Coach Clayton relinquished the floor to Blake, who led everyone in the Lord's Prayer. Then he raised his head, smiling. "As you all know," he said, "Louie's makes the best pizza in town, but for this special occasion tonight, pizza didn't seem quite appropriate. So, Cody and I got with Mike, and we formulated an idea."

Blake looked back toward the kitchen. "Mike, if you would, please," he called.

Mike stepped forward, carrying a large circular platter. On the platter sat several plates—topped with metal covers—the kind Cody had seen used at sports banquets in the past. Following Mike were three members of his restaurant staff, then a host of volunteers, including Robyn and Jessica Adams.

"I need to ask you," Blake said, raising his voice, "to keep the covers on your plates until everyone is served. No peeking."

Blake paused while the waitstaff finished serving. Then he addressed his audience again. "As I was saying, pizza wouldn't be the appropriate cuisine for this particular occasion, so, on the count of three, if everyone would lift the covers and reveal tonight's special menu item. One . . . two . . . three!"

Across a booth from Chop, Cody studied his friend as he lifted his plate cover, a smile stretching across his face.

"Pork chops!" Drew barked from a nearby table. "We're having pork chops in honor of Pork Chop!"

"That's right," Blake proclaimed. "So, if you would, please, all of you, let's raise our pork chops in salute to the one, the only, Pork Chop!"

Dozens of pork chops were thrust in the air, amid cheers and laughter.

Cody looked to his friend again. "You kill me, dawg," Chop said, wagging his head. "You really kill me. Thanks."

The pork chops, along with mashed potatoes and applesauce, were followed by Louie's famous dessert pizzas—cookie-dough crusts topped with cherries, blueberries, or cinnamon and sugar—then drizzled with white icing.

Cody took one bite of his third slice of dessert pizza, then set it down and shoved his plate away from him. *It's too bad that eating this stuff isn't an Ultimate Athlete event,* he thought, smiling. *I might actually have a chance. But I feel like I'm ready to pop. And I'm not going to be able to compete well next week if I gain ten pounds before the competition. Besides, it's time to start thinking about The Speech.*

While helping Blake and Coach Clayton organize Chop's official send-off, Cody had asked if he could say a few words to conclude the evening. Now, as he stepped warily to the front of Louie's Pizza, he began to question the wisdom of his request. *It will be a total buzz kill,* he warned himself, *if you get up there and fumble your words like a greased football—or start crying or something.*

He waited until the room grew church-prayer-time quiet. "I don't have much to say," he began, "just thanks, Chop. Thanks for all the beatings you saved me from, ever since third grade. Thanks for always having my back, on the field, on the court, everywhere. But most of all ... well, Proverbs says that there's a kind of friend who sticks closer than a brother. Thanks for being that kind of friend to me. My *best* friend."

Cody nodded gratefully when Blake stood and began applauding furiously. The rest of the room followed suit.

Cody helped Blake collect the last of the wadded-up napkins, pork chop bones, and empty soda cups. Pork Chop had left five minutes ago, giving Cody a fierce hug and a sincere "Thanks, dawg. You're my boy."

"You okay, Cody?" Blake asked, holding a plastic trash bag open while Cody deposited two plates' worth of leftovers into it.

Cody sighed. "I don't know, B. You know, I've done a lot of hard things in sports, playing through injuries, competing against older, stronger, more experienced guys. I've even had a couple of fights. But nothing's as hard as saying good-bye to someone you care about. I had to do it with my mom. And now, again, with Chop. I know God will be beside me all the way, but I just don't know how I'm going to survive this. I can't picture my life without my mom and my best friend in it. I can't see it, you know?"

Blake smiled at him warmly. "But God does know. He already sees it. That's the important thing. And you need to keep one thing in mind."

"What's that, B?"

"Both of those hard good-byes? Neither one of them is permanent."

Chapter 5
The Ultimate Pain

Cody handed the chocolate bar to Beth, who reclined on her bed, in the Martin master bedroom, at least three pillows piled like pancakes under her shoulders. "Thanks so much, Cody," she said. "I really nee ... I mean, the baby really needed this."

Cody grinned at her. "You or the baby boy need anything else?"

"No. Not right now. But thank you for asking. You have been so good to me these last couple of weeks. I feel like such a slug, but doctor's orders are doctor's orders, I guess."

"It's no problem, Beth. I'll do whatever you need. Just ask."

"Well, right now I ask that you get off your feet.

You've got a big competition starting in two days. You need to rest up."

And, Cody thought, as he closed the bedroom door behind him, *I have a killer of a good-bye to say this afternoon.*

Cody stirred his triple-thick vanilla shake with his straw, noting that the drink wasn't even "single-thick" anymore, after nearly an hour. Normally, he would have sucked down one of his favorite beverages in less than five minutes, but this afternoon, with Chop slumped in the booth across from him, he found his appetite had deserted him.

"What's wrong?" Chop queried. "The Double D using inferior ice cream now?"

Cody smiled sadly. "What about you? You've taken, like, one sip of root beer the whole time."

Chop sighed heavily. "It's really happening, little bro. Doug will be here in a few minutes, and we'll start the drive to Tennessee. Go figure. This is probably our last meal together here, and we're both too bummed to eat anything."

Cody tried to laugh but managed only a weak sigh. "This stinks," he said.

Chop nodded weakly. "It stinks like the Mill Creek locker room. Remember that?"

"Yeah. That was a room in need of a plumber."

Cody pushed his shake away. He sat back in the booth and studied his friend's wounded face. The silence between them reminded him of the silence between thunderclaps during a violent storm.

Presently, a bald man in a tight black T-shirt and expensive-looking jeans appeared at their booth. *Where have I seen this dude?* Cody asked himself. *He looks kinda familiar.*

"Mr. Sanders," Pork Chop bellowed, "look at you, bro! You finally got that pelt off your head!"

Smiling, Mr. Sanders ran a hand over his smooth, pale skull. "And I shaved the fringes," he explained. "Of course, I don't need to shave up-top; genetics took care of that for me."

"You look good, Mr. Sanders," Cody offered. "I didn't recognize you at first, without the toupee."

"I didn't recognize me the first time I looked in the mirror. But, Cody, remember when Blake subbed for Pastor Taylor and he preached that sermon called 'Keeping It Real'? Well, that helped me realize that I definitely wasn't keeping it real. Then when you shared about Mr. Porter here at the end of the service—"

"Wait a minute!" Chop interrupted. "What exactly did you share about me, dawg?"

Cody fidgeted for a moment. "Well," he began, "remember this spring—when you swore off all of the performance-enhancing supplements and decided to go natural? I was proud of you for that. And I just wanted to tell people. Especially because a lot of Crossroads people pray for you all the time."

Chop nodded. "I guess that's kinda cool. I'm not sure how I feel about you puttin' my business out there, but—"

"If I may," Mr. Sanders interjected, "Cody told everyone how proud he was of you, Deke. But he didn't mention you by name. Of course, many of us knew whom he was talking about. I need you to know, though, that what Cody shared about you helped inspire me to shed that awful rug. I gave it to Mrs. Leadbetter, for her cat, Buttercup. Buttercup hissed at it at first, but now I understand that she loves it—plays with it all day, sleeps with it all night."

"Well," Pork Chop said, a smile creasing his face, "I guess it's all good in the 'hood then. I mean, look at you, Mr. Sanders. The fitted T, the Diesel jeans, the Reebok kicks. I mean, go on, playa!"

Mr. Sanders began backing away from the booth, apologetically. "Of course, I really should be going; I didn't mean to interrupt—"

Chop and Cody erupted in laughter. "No, no," Chop said imploringly. "I don't want you to go away. That was a compliment. I was just telling you that your look is junk."

"Junk?" Mr. Sanders said, with a hopeless shrug.

"You look cool, Mr. Sanders," Cody added. "You look good." He noticed that Mr. Sander's head had turned from ghostly white to stoplight red.

"Uh ... th-thank you," Mr. Sanders stammered. He placed a hand on Chop's shoulder. "Go with God, young man," he said. "And, keep, uh, keep it real."

"Thank you, sir," Chop replied. "I will."

"There's Doug's Camry pulling in," Chop said, breaking a near-five-minute silence. "So, I guess this is it. Anything I can do before I go?"

Cody raised his eyes from a gash in the tabletop. "You know what I really want you to do? Come back."

"I'll come back someday, Code. Maybe we'll both go to college together. Up in Boulder. Or maybe Fort Collins."

"That's not what I mean by 'come back,' and I think you know it. I want you to come back to God. Even if we can't sit together in church and youth group like back in the day, if I could just know that down in Tennessee you've found a church and stuff—"

Chop tilted his head back. When he spoke, Cody couldn't tell whether it was annoyance or something else in his voice. "Look, Code, I do feel this pull back to God, back to church sometimes. But there's something just as strong pulling me in another direction. I just don't know that I believe everything that you believe. I'm not sure I can be like you and Robyn and Drew. I'm not sure I want to be. It's like there's this big tug-of-war going on, and it's killin' me."

"You always say that tug-of-war is fun."

Chop took a halfhearted sip of his root beer. "Not when *I'm* the rope," he sighed.

Cody slid out of his side of the booth and held the door for Chop. As they walked across the parking lot, Cody saw Doug Porter nod at him from the driver's seat of his Camry. Somehow he knew that Doug would stay in the car, at least for a while, to give his brother a chance to say good-bye.

Cody stood about three feet from his friend. It reminded him of how he faced the captain of the opposing team before a game.

"What are you thinking right now, little brother?" Chop asked, his voice barely a whisper.

"I don't know if you really want to know. I don't know if I really want to tell you, if I'm even supposed to tell you."

"C'mon, Code. That's the one thing about you—you've always told me the truth. You've always kept it real."

"You might think it's weird."

Chop shrugged. "*Life* is weird. My pops is a white country-boy farmer; my moms is a sista from Five Points. I own a 'doo rag *and* a Stetson. My best friend in the world is a skinny white dude. I like hip-hop music, but I like country too sometimes. So, I can handle weird. So, come on with it."

"Well, Chop, to tell you the truth, I have been thinking about heaven most of the day. How it's a place of perfect happiness. Perfect—that's a big word, you know."

"Yeah?"

"Well, what I'm wondering—what's eating a hole in my gut lately—is how can I be perfectly happy in heaven if you're not there? I mean, it's not, like, theologically correct for me to feel this way, but it's honestly how I feel."

Chop bowed his head. "Dawg, I don't know what to say. What you just told me—that's heavy. I wish I could say something to make you feel better, but I just can't right now. All I can say is keep praying for me."

"You know I will, Chop. Like a starving man praying for a scrap of food."

Chop's good-bye hug was fierce and quick. He marched to his brother's car, not with his usual slow, loose jock's saunter, but the hurried, quick-stepped gait of a businessman late for a meeting. Once inside the car, he buried his face in his hands. Doug curled an arm around his shoulder as he backed out of the lot.

Cody felt a few tears escape and slide down his face. "Please, God," he whispered, "don't let Chop go."

He thought for a moment about clarifying his prayer—that he knew his friend had to move and it was futile to ask for anything different. But he knew God understood exactly what he meant by 'don't let Chop go.'

Chapter 6

Ten Battles, One War

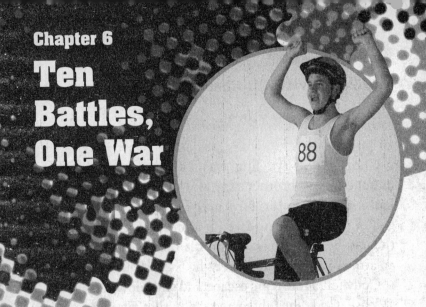

Okay," Coach Clayton said, addressing the four Grant High sophomores-to-be halfcircled around him, "let's start strong. I'll do my best to help all of you, but there's a lot going on here. Blake Randall—ya'll know Cody's youth pastor, right?—he'll be up here a little later to help me out. And, speaking of Cody Martin, I'll have my cell turned on all the time, just in case your daddy calls about any further pregnancy complications."

Cody nodded. "Beth's been fine since she's been on bed rest, so I think we'll be all right. She's just bummed that she can't be here to watch."

"Well," Coach Clayton said, "you just go out there and get after it, and I'll personally describe it for her later. Now, the 100 meters is first. All of y'all go get your stretch on. I don't want any of you yay-hoos pulling a hammy right from the get-go."

Event 1: The 100 Meters

Cody drew lane one for the opening event. *Good,* he thought. *This way, if I'm gettin' smoked too bad, I'll just veer into the infield and get lost in the crowd.*

He adjusted his starting blocks, trying to remember the last time he had used them. Probably back in seventh grade when Dylan had talked him into trying the high hurdles.

He surveyed the competition. Antwan Clay was two lanes over. He exchanged nods with his Central opponent, thinking, *Well, that takes the mystery out of who will win this heat. 'Twan can flat out fly. And check this out—there's Locke out in lane five. I don't think I can beat him in a sprint. This is getting depressing. But I gotta remember, I'm competing against the clock here, not the other guys. It's all about the points. Until the last event, of course.*

"To your marks, gentlemen," ordered the starter. Cody focused on the thin strip of lane ahead of him. He placed his hands carefully on the track's spongy surface, willing himself to focus on the next command, which would be "Set!" followed by the crack of the starter's pistol.

At the sound of the gun, Cody felt Clay explode from the blocks. In response, he launched his body forward, trying to match Clay's quick strides.

Halfway through the race, Clay began to pull away, but Cody sensed he was in the hunt for second place. He fought the temptation to swivel his head to his right to survey the other runners.

As he crossed the finish line, his peripheral vision caught Locke, trying to out-lean him. *I think I got him*, he thought. *That's pretty cool.*

He pulled on his sweats and headed for the stands to find Coach Clayton. "I had you in second, dawg," the coach said, smiling. "About a twelve seven."

"That's pretty good, isn't it?" Cody asked hopefully. "I mean, for a guy who specializes in middle distances."

"It's not a bad start, Mr. Martin. The Olympic team won't be calling, but it'll do. I had a clock on Macy; he did a twelve nine in the first heat and took third. Nakamura scorched an eleven four in the second heat, but he was way ahead of everybody else. Bottom line—I think you're in the hunt. Now, go get ready to heave the shot. And, dawg, for the love of Brian Oldfield, please don't drop it on your toe."

Event 2: The Shot Put

Whoa, Cody thought, as he nestled the shot put below the right side of his jaw, *it's hard to believe something only as big as a grapefruit can be so heavy. What's inside this thing—the stuff neutron stars are made of?*

He eyed the closest of a series of parallel curved chalk lines in the sand ahead of him as he stood on the concrete surface of the shot put ring. *Okay*, he urged himself, *just try to get it to that first line.*

Trying to mimic Pork Chop's form, Cody crouched, then scooted toward the front of the ring, when he felt his left foot nudge the raised curb at the ring's edge, he lunged and thrust his right arm forward, launching the metal orb up and out. He heard himself grunt from the exertion and was grateful Robyn wasn't around to hear it. *She'd think I was a caveman*, he surmised. *And Robyn no-likey cavemen.*

He studied the spot where the shot put plopped in the moist sand, about a foot short of the first line. *Oh well*, he consoled himself, *there are a few craters not as far out as mine—and at least I didn't drop the shot on my toe.*

Cody scratched on his next two attempts, his momentum causing him to stumble over the curb and out of the ring. He stayed to watch Clay beat his only good mark by four feet, then trudged away, wondering, *Will I get, like, negative points for such a weak toss?*

Event 3: The 400 Meters

Time to get busy now, Cody urged himself. *The quarter-mile—this is more in my wheelhouse. I bet I've run a million quarters in track practice. Coach Clayton loves 'em. Probably because they are gut-busters, and he's a sadist.*

He jumped a few times off of both feet, eyeing the competition. Clay, thankfully, was not in this heat. But Cabrera was, way out in lane eight, seven lanes away.

With the report of the starter's pistol, Cody was off. He pumped his arms, striving to get to top speed quickly. He passed a stocky runner in lane three before he hit the first turn. Locke, running too tightly in lane two, was toast midway through the turn. Halfway down the backstretch, Cody looked right, noting that he was stride for stride with Berringer in lane four.

In basketball and football, Berringer typically beat him during the early suicides and gassers, respectively. But Berringer was notorious for fading later on.

Cody risked a prolonged glance at his teammate. Berringer was clearly straining, his face frozen in a pained grimace.

Cody powered through the second turn, shortening his stride and leaning toward the inside portion of his lane. The inexperienced runners would, no doubt, drift to the outside of their lanes, maybe even step into an opponent's lane and get disqualified. This was a chance to make up for the weak shot put effort.

As he burst into the final straightaway, Cody sensed he was in first place. *Hang on!* he commanded himself. He heard the roar of the crowd swell, and somehow he knew Cabrera was challenging him, making one final surge. Panic rippled down his spine when he noticed, out of the corner of his eye, the compact runner drawing even with him, then edging ahead.

Cody lengthened his stride, straining toward the finish line. Cabrera was tying up too—maybe there was time to regain the lead.

"Crud!" Cody spat as he saw Cabrera take the finish-line tape across his chest, one stride ahead of him. He angled toward his foe and extended his hand. "Good finish," he gasped.

Cabrera hesitated a moment, then accepted the gesture.

Cody scanned the stands. He saw Coach Clayton, flashing him five fingers, then six. *Hmm*, Cody thought, *a fifty-six-second quarter. And it's not even track season. I'll take that any day.*

Event 4: The Long Jump

Cody sprinted down the runway, then leaped off his right leg, propelling himself up and out, over the well-raked sandpit.

He knew he had hit the board perfectly at the end of the runway, avoiding the shame of an official raising a red flag and hollering "Scratch!"

The only problem, he thought as he landed in the soft sand, *is that I had a great takeoff from my right leg and I wanted to jump off my left leg. How in the world could my steps be off so badly? I practiced my run-up at least a half-dozen times.*

On his next attempt, he jumped off the proper leg, but launched himself from six inches behind the board, costing himself valuable distance.

"Sixteen feet, seven inches," said an official after studying his metal measuring tape. "Not bad, young man."

Cody was inclined to agree with the official— until he saw Clay and Macy top seventeen feet on consecutive jumps. Even Drew bettered Cody's mark, hitting the board perfectly on a sixteen feet, eight inches effort.

Cody adjusted his run-up for his third and final leap. More correctly, he overadjusted. Two-thirds of the way to the board, he realized he was going to have to chop his steps and slow considerably to get off a fair jump. He decided to let his one decent jump stand. He ran over the board, through the sand, and kept right on going to the basketball courts.

Event 5: One-on-One Basketball

"Go easy on me, Code," Drew said. "I'm out of my element here."

Cody forced a laugh as he stood at the top of the key in the Denver Northwest gymnasium, watching the action going on around the five other baskets.

"Gentlemen," a bulldog-faced referee said, handing a basketball to Cody. "You know the drill—the game is to ten, by ones. Or a ten-minute time limit, whichever comes first. I'll do my best to call fouls, but try to keep it clean. I don't want to have to spend the next several minutes blowing my whistle and breaking up shoving matches."

The referee didn't blow his whistle once during the ensuing seven minutes. Drew was on Cody like an overcoat, but his defense, while aggressive and unsettlingly close, wasn't dirty. But it wasn't enough to keep Cody from getting one clear shot at the basket. Hence, the one to zero score.

I'm lucky Drew couldn't throw the ball in the ocean if he was standin' on the shore, Cody thought, drawing in a deep breath and eyeing the clock. *Or I'd be down by about five buckets, instead of up by one.*

Cody rebounded his own errant midrange jumper, then head-faked Drew. His friend bit on the fake, and Cody drove hard to the basket, knowing Drew would recover quickly and be on his back like a predator. Therefore, he panicked and hurried his shot. The ball dripped off the front rim.

Drew charged in for the rebound, then retreated to the free throw line on the change of possession. Cody expected Drew to drive for a layup of his own, but instead he elevated and fired on off-balance jumper.

The ball smacked hard off the glass backboard … and slipped neatly through the net.

"Didn't hear you call glass on that one," Cody chided playfully as he positioned himself behind the free throw line.

Thirty seconds remained on the clock. Cody knew what Coach Clayton would be telling him if he were here—"Milk the clock, dawg. Get it down to two or three seconds, then take a good shot. End this thing—you don't want to go to a five-minute overtime with a guy who has a motor like Drew Phelps. The boy never gets tired!"

Cody dribbled patiently, watching the seconds on the LED clock click down to eight. Then he lowered his shoulder and knifed toward the basket. Drew danced into his path, cutting off the drive.

Cody turned his back to Drew, feeling the pressure of his friend's bony arm between his hip bones. He began counting down the final seconds in his head . . . *six, five*—

Suddenly, the pressure on his back vanished. Drew was coming around for a steal. He saw a long arm snake around on his right and poke the ball away.

No overtime, no overtime, Cody chanted in his head as he lurched forward, making sure he kept his body between Drew and the ball. He scooped up the ball near the sideline, turned, and flung a desperate one-handed shot toward the basket.

The ball jitterbugged along the rim and bounced away, just as Cody half-expected it would.

What he didn't expect is what Drew did next.

After racing the shot back to the rim, Drew propelled himself upward, impressing Cody with his vertical leap. Cody knew his friend was going to collect the rebound, but he took consolation in knowing there wouldn't be time to escort the ball back to the free throw line and get a shot off in the next second or so.

"We're going to overtime," Cody muttered disgustedly. "There's no doubt about it."

There was no overtime.

In his zeal to snare the errant shot, Drew tipped Cody's shot back toward the basket, like a volleyball player dinking a shot over a leaping defender. The ball climbed over the rim and dropped through the net.

The referee ran immediately to the scorer's table and began conferring with a man who was running the clock and the scoreboard.

"The basket's good," he said, turning toward Cody and pointing. "You get the win."

"Wouldn't you know it," Drew said, clapping Cody across the back. "I finally get the blasted ball to go in the basket, and I do it for the wrong guy!"

I can't remember how many points we get for each basketball win, Cody thought, *shaking his head in relief. But I earned 'em on that one.*

Cody's second opponent was an arrow-thin blond kid from Denver, sporting more piercings than Cody had ever seen—at least on a guy.

Pierce Boy bolted to a five to zero lead, all on long-range jumpers, all with Cody right in his face.

As he watched one of his own shots from the baseline clang off the far side of the rim, Cody smacked his hands together in frustration. *Guess I'm gonna have to write this one off as a loss*, he thought. *This guy is shooting lights-out, and I can't buy a bucket.*

He trudged back toward the free throw line, wondering if it was even worth elevating to try to block Pierce Boy's next shot.

"Dawg!" a voice behind him rumbled. "Don't you give up. Don't you even think about giving up!"

Cody whipped his head around. "Chop?" he said, blinking as he saw his friend standing ten feet away. "Wha—"

Chop wagged his head sternly. "Later, dawg," he ordered. "Focus on the game."

Cody positioned himself in front of Pierce Boy, who took the ball from the referee and flashed Cody a cocky grin.

Cody watched the grin vanish as he slapped the ball away and darted to the basket for an easy layup.

On his next possession, Pierce Boy missed his first shot. Cody corralled the rebound, then burned his opponent with a crossover dribble and another layup."

"Try that mess again!" Pierce Boy sneered the next time Cody held the ball.

Okay, Cody thought. He crossed over from his left hand to his right, then back to the left. Pierce Boy was beaten so badly that he didn't even bother to pursue.

"Whoo-weee!" Coach Clayton said, as he joined Pork Chop to watch the action. "For the love of Allen Iverson, that was a sweet double-crossover!"

Cody gave them both a quick smile.

He gave them a longer smile when a left-handed fade-away gave him a ten to five comeback win.

Pierce Boy refused to shake his hand, a dis that Pork Chop noticed. "That's okay, ya sorry sport," he chided. "My boy shouldn't shake your hand anyway—that lousy shooting touch of yours might be contagious! And by the way, your mama called; she wants her jewelry back!"

Chop appeared to be reloading for another insult, when Blake grabbed him by the wrist and pulled him away.

Cody had time only to exchange quick fist-pounds with Chop before he was called to his next game, which pitted him against Shervin, a distance-running specialist from Maranatha Christian School. Like Drew, Shervin was a tenacious defender but a poor shooter. And he lacked Drew's decent vertical leap. Cody blocked five of his shots on the way to a ten to three rout.

"Three up, no down!" Chop said after the win, chest-bumping Cody so hard that he staggered backward. "That's the way to handle your business out there, dawg!"

Cody stood, slack-jawed. "I still can't believe you're here. I don't get it."

Chop smiled warmly. "Well, little brother, here's how it went down, We're not even to the state line—

not even to Burlington yet—and I tell Doug, 'I just can't let my boy compete up in Denver without me in his corner.' Doug groans and grumbles for a while, but then he calls our pops on his cell, and we work out a compromise. Bottom line—I'm here for the next two days. I got your back all the way through this thing, Code."

Cody drank in a deep breath. "I don't know what to say. Thanks, Chop. This is unbelievable."

"What's unbelievable," Coach Clayton said, draping his long arms around Cody and Chop's shoulders, "is that you're in third place, dawg. Within spittin' distance of Clay and Cabrera."

"What about Dylan?" Cody asked. "I thought for sure he'd be up among the leaders."

Coach Clayton shook his head. "He scratched on all three long jump tries. No points at all. He's cooked, I'm afraid. And you will be too, if you don't get your skinny carcass over to yonder side hoop for your next game."

Cody stayed with opponent number four, Antwan Clay, for the first five minutes. But, as the game wore on, he found Clay too quick off the dribble. The final score was respectable, ten to seven, but Cody made a mental note to work on his footwork before and during the upcoming hoops season.

Cody's final foe was a hulking six feet, three inches farm kid from Calhan. He backed Cody into the paint with ease, but missed enough easy shots to keep the game close. Clinging to a nine to eight lead in the game's final minute, Cody jab-stepped left, then drove right. He sensed the Calhan kid right behind him, so instead of shooting a traditional layup from the right side, he slid under the basket and executed a reverse layup from the left. Angry at being fooled, Kid Calhan slapped the backboard with both hands, which would have given Cody the winning basket via goaltending, even if his shot hadn't trickled in.

Four wins, one loss, Cody thought as he headed for the weight room. *I was afraid it would be the other way around.*

Event 6: The Bench Press

"One hundred forty-seven pounds," called out a muscle-bound official in a tight-fitting, white T-shirt. "So you'll be lifting 145 pounds. Remember to keep your hips on the bench at all times—and the bar must touch your chest on each rep."

Cody nodded as his eyes scanned the room. In a far corner, Cabrera grunted as he strained for one final repetition, his fourth or fifth. On a closer bench, two burly spotters lifted 125 pounds off of Shervin's chest.

He hadn't managed a single rep. In fact, his pool-cue arms seemed to offer no resistance when he began his first attempt. It looked to Cody like the weight was free-falling onto Shervin's concave torso.

As he positioned himself on the bench vacated by Shervin, Cody was grateful for all the time he and Chop had spent in the Grant High weight room, not to mention the hours in the Porters' basement-turned-workout-facility. He was also grateful that this portion of the competition was based on each athlete's ability to lift his own body weight— measuring pound-for-pound strength, not pure brute power. The guy from Calhan looked like he could bench-press a horse. And Dylan was already threatening to join Grant's two hundred-pound BP club.

Cody accepted the bar from the spotters, and after making sure he was balanced, he slowly lowered the bar, inflating his chest like a balloon at the same time. When he felt the steel pressing on his breastbone, he groaned and thrust his arms upward.

"That's one!" a spotter barked.

Cody felt his left arm quivering as he lowered the bar on his second attempt. *This is trouble*, he thought. He allowed the bar to bounce a bit off of his chest, hoping it wouldn't be enough to have the rep disallowed. The tiny bit of momentum helped him get the bar past his "sticking point," and with some ungainly straining, he was able to lock his elbows and give himself a grand total of two repetitions.

"Good effort," one of the spotters called to him. Then, lowering his voice, the spotter added, "You were real close to having me DQ that second rep. Don't get in the habit of bouncing steel off your chest, especially as you start throwing around bigger and bigger weights. You don't even want to know what it's like to bruise your sternum."

Cody nodded solemnly.

"Not bad, dawg," Coach Clayton said, leading Cody to a locker room. "Macy didn't get a single rep. Neither did that yay-hoo with all the piercings. And Drew, bless his pea-pickin' heart, got only one. And that was the single longest, most excruciating bench press in the history of weight lifting. He got that bar up on pure willpower—'cuz it sure wasn't on form or skill."

"I have a feeling Drew'll make up for it in the bike race," Cody said.

Event 7: 20-Mile Bike Race

"Too bad the rules say no drafting," Drew said, adjusting his cycling helmet. "You could tuck in behind me and have a wind resistance-free ride."

"Uh, Phelps," Cody said, "you're assuming I can stay anywhere near you. It's hard to draft off a guy who's a mile ahead."

Drew frowned. "I don't think I can beat you by a whole mile. It's only a twenty-mile ride."

Well, Cody reasoned several minutes later, *Drew was right about the distance between us. It's not even close to a mile. It's more like two miles. Man, the way he took off at the start, it seemed like his bike had a motor — which in a way it does. It's Drew-powered.*

Cody looked at the small computer mounted on the handlebars of his 12-speed. The speedometer read eighteen miles an hour, exactly where Drew told him he should be on the flat portions of the course.

As he finished his third lap of the five-mile course, Shervin drew even with him, then left him behind on a gentle one hundred-yard hill.

Just like that little Winters kid on the last lap, Cody thought disgustedly. *Oh, well, there can't be more than a dozen or so guys ahead of me, and there are more than three hundred in the competition. And I haven't seen Clay, Keenan Jones, Macy, or Cabrera.*

With about three miles to go, Berringer made a charge. Cody felt his spirits deflate when Berringer rose up out of his saddle and powered by him. *Whoa*, Cody thought, *the Bear's looking strong. He's gonna be tough come football season. Look at those man-calves. I know what Coach Clayton would be saying right now—"Son, those aren't calves; them are steers!"*

Unfortunately for Cody's teammate, Berringer's left man-calf cramped badly two miles from the finish.

"It's like I stepped in a bear trap," he complained as Cody pulled alongside of him. "I think I can finish, but I'm gonna have to back off."

"You sure you don't need help?" Cody offered.

"Nah, I'm cool. You keep going. Clayton thinks you can medal in this thing. So don't wait for me."

Reluctantly, Cody increased his cadence. After a minute or so, he looked behind. Berringer saw him and waved him on.

One mile from the finish, he saw Cabrera on the side of the course, cursing and banging his small hand pump against the frame of his bike.

Cody coasted to Cabrera's side and dismounted. "Flat?" he said.

He could see the frustration in Cabrera's eyes. "It's not all the way flat, but it's way low. It's messin' up my rhythm. Then this stupid pump—"

"Here," Cody said, removing his pump from his bike frame. "Use mine."

"What's with you, Martin? You're burnin' time here. Or are you so far out of the competition that you don't even care?"

"Not exactly," Cody sighed. "Look, take my pump. It works great. You can get it back to me at the finish."

Cody squirmed under Cabrera's suspicious gaze. "What if you get a flat, Martin?"

Cody shrugged. "That's a chance I'll have to take."

Cabrera spat on the asphalt. "Well, thanks, I guess. But if I see you pulled over with a flat, don't expect me to stop to help you—not even with your own pump. No mercy."

"I'm not asking for mercy," Cody said, feeling a stab of frustration as a pack of four riders whipped by. He placed his left foot in the toe clip and pushed off with his right. Moments later, he was back up to full speed. He had almost reeled the pack in when he saw the finish area. As he powered across the line, he wondered how much time he had lost helping Cabrera—and how many points that had cost him. But he also remembered his father's words about what truly made an Ultimate Competitor.

Event 8: The High Jump

After landing on the high jump bar, rather than soaring over it on his first two attempts, Cody slapped the stop-sign-red mat angrily before scrambling off of it. "I'm gonna no-height in this thing," he muttered, "which means I am toast in the competition. I can't believe Chop turned around and came back for this."

Cody pulled on his sweatpants and began to pace the infield. Presently, he felt Chop by his side. "If you make one crack about 'White Man's Disease' Chop, I swear I'm gonna lose it."

Chop smiled sadly. "I wouldn't bust on you at a time like this, dawg. Besides, you got decent ups. Clayton says your problem is that your Fosbury flop is too much flop and not enough Fosbury."

"Well, then," Cody snapped, "Coach should try to go over a five-foot-high bar—backwards. It's not as easy as fallin' off a log, you know!"

"I know," Chop said nodding. "I never realized how hard high-jumping is until we started messing around after track practice a few years ago. It isn't easy—getting your whole body over that bar. But it can be done."

Cody held his arms out imploringly, palms toward the sky. "You mind telling me how? You're a high jump expert now, are ya?"

"Code, you need to chill. You believe that Jesus calmed that stormy sea, like we heard back in Sunday school?"

"Of course I do."

"Then maybe you need to ask him to calm your insides."

Cody smiled at his friend. "Yeah, you're right. And, you know, for somebody who said church was a big drag, you sure remember a lot about it."

Chop returned Cody's smile. "There's something else I remember. Remember when we were goofin' around on the high jump back in eighth grade and Alston comes running at the bar, head-on, like he's gonna hurdle it or something?"

Cody frowned. "Yeah. So?"

"Soooooo, he gets to the bar, but instead of hurdling it, he plants his foot and somersaults over it. We all think that's cool, so we start doing it too. You caught some big air jumpin' that way, remember?"

"I guess I did, but the bar was only set at, like, four and a half feet. That's a long way from five."

"Yeah, but you're older now, and stronger. And smarter. Smart enough to listen to your best friend."

"Martin, from Grant," Cody heard an official near the high jump area call, "third and final attempt."

Cody felt many competitors' eyes on him as he began his straight-on run-up. Everyone else, whether using the Fosbury flop, the western roll, or the scissors, approached the bar from either the right or left side, carving a banana-shaped run-up.

They must think I'm nuts, Cody figured as he propelled himself off his left foot and curled his body over the bar. He could tell from Chop's whoops that he had cleared it.

The "Pork Chop Dive" got Cody over the next height, five feet, two inches. He bowed out at five feet, three inches, but only Locke, Dylan, Clay, Macy, and one or two others remained.

"You're still in the top five, Mr. Martin," Coach Clayton said, "and the next two events should be two of your best."

Event 9: The Obstacle Course

"I've seen courses like these on TV," Drew said, "but you don't realize how high that wall is until you see it up close."

Cody nodded and swallowed hard. "And it's sadistic that they put it at the end of the course. I wish we could get it out of the way earlier."

The word circulating around the course was that Cabrera had turned in the fastest time of the day, at just over a minute and a half. Clay, conversely, had stumbled over one of the three hurdles and done a face-plant in the thick grass before scrambling to his feet, only to run right through the twelve-foot water jump, saddling himself with a five-second penalty.

As Cody waited his turn in line, he felt a finger poking into his ribs. "Hey, Phelps," he said to the owner of the finger. "You get through it okay?"

"I had a clean run, but that wall nearly killed me. Listen, you gotta get some momentum when you run up to that thing. I had no 'mo,' so I had to climb the rope attached to the wall from nearly a dead stop. Took me forever."

"What you should do," Dylan chimed in from behind Drew, "is be like Locke. He didn't even use the rope. He just leaped, grabbed the top of the wall, and pulled himself over."

"I don't know," said Cody, whistling through his teeth for emphasis. "Locke has, probably, four inches on me. And the top of that wall is ten feet! As high as the basketball rim, as high as a football crossbar. I can barely graze the bottom of the crossbar, 'cuz it's so thick. But I can't quite touch the rim. I tried the last time Chop and I shot buckets."

"Well," Dylan said, "maybe you'll get a burst of adrenaline."

"Yeah," Cody replied, "or maybe I'll grow wings."

Cody found himself paired against Keenan Jones. *Wonderful*, he thought, *this is gonna be payback. KJ's gonna school me on the obstacle course to pay me back for all the times I've schooled him in basketball.*

Jones nodded at Cody, then dug his feet into the grass and waited for the whistle that would begin the race.

Cody stood, his hands swinging at his sides. On the shrill, rippling blast of the starter's whistle, he was off;

quick, choppy strides carrying him to about ten square feet of netting, held only a couple feet off the ground by a series of small tent pegs. He slid onto his stomach and using his elbows and knees, wriggled under the netting.

Once through, he popped to his feet and began negotiating a set of twenty black rubber car tires, placed side by side. He had done this drill hundreds of times in football practice, and, using high, choppy steps, he danced his way through with ease.

He guessed he had a five-yard lead on Jones as he drove his shoulder into a blocking sled, plowing it ten yards across a white line painted in the grass. A series of monkey bars was next. *This was easier when I was six*, Cody thought as he gripped the cold metal bars and pulled his way through obstacle number four.

The water jump was next, and Cody leaped so hard that he nearly stumbled upon landing, a good foot beyond the edge of the rectangular pit filled with coffee-colored water.

Then came the hurdles. Jones, a strong hurdler, pulled ahead of Cody at the third and final hurdle. Now it was a forty-yard sprint to the deep-blue wall, dubbed the Blue Monster by the competitors.

Jones was flying, but Cody let him go. Instead, he focused on the distance to the wall. *If I come to the Monster in stride*, he thought, *I'm gonna try something.*

Jones was already halfway up the wall when Cody approached like Batman. About six feet from the wall, Cody launched himself up and forward off his right foot. Then he planted his left foot about four feet from the bottom and channeled the momentum into a lunge for the top of the wall.

He felt his right hand grip the wall's top— precariously, just above the second knuckle of his middle finger and forefinger of his right hand.

Fear clamped his heart as he felt himself losing his grip. Frantically, he pawed for the rope with his left hand. He felt its rough surface scrape his hand as he grabbed it and tugged. The little boost helped him secure a better grip on the wall. He released his hold on the rope and placed his left hand near his right.

He hung there for just a moment, long enough to draw in one mighty breath. Then he pulled himself up, his feet digging and scraping for some traction on the Blue Monster.

He was able to get his right elbow atop the wall, then the left one. He swung his right leg up and over, shifting his body weight.

Now straddling the wall, he took a quick peek over the other side before lowering himself over it and releasing his grip.

"Yes!" he panted as he dropped to the padding at the wall's base.

"No!" he yelped, as he felt a hot needle of pain stab into his left ankle.

Event 10: The 5-Kilometer Run

Coach Clayton handed Cody a bottle of sports drink. "Gulp this down, dawg," he said. "You're gonna need it."

Cody looked on nervously as he watched Locke begin his run, using long, loping strides. "Keenan Jones," he heard an announcer say, "be ready to begin your run in thirty-eight seconds."

"This is weird," Cody observed, "everybody taking off at different times."

"I kinda like it, the way they've handicapped it," Coach Clayton said. "It makes it a true competition— using everyone's points in the previous events to determine who starts when. And it makes the last event truly significant. Whoever wins the run, wins the whole enchilada. That could be you, dawg."

"Really, Coach? You really think I have a chance? I mean, Phelps, he's a machine. He's gonna tear this course up."

"Maybe," the coach said, nodding and rubbing his chin. "But you're gonna have a whale of a lead on him. A good minute and a half."

Cody half-snorted. "As if that's gonna be enough!"

"I don't know, dawg. Ol' Flash Phelps is hurtin'. His body has taken a pounding. And that dad-gummed Blue Monster nearly did him in."

"Cody Martin," the announcer barked. "Seventeen seconds. Sixteen, fifteen—"

Cody exchanged fist-pounds with his coach, then Pork Chop, and trotted to the start line. He waited until he heard "Three, two, one!" before darting from the line. The stabbing pain in his ankle had disappeared a few minutes after the obstacle course, but he had felt a mild twinge or two while loosening up for the 5-kilometer run.

He felt like saying a silent prayer of thanks every time his left foot touched down, then pushed off. *Just three miles*, he prayed. *Please let the pain be gone for the next three miles*.

He passed the mile mark, as a timer droned, ". . . five-fifty-two, five-fifty-three—"

At a mile and a half, the pain returned, and it was angry. Cody shortened his stride, trying to step as gingerly as possible. He had just passed Locke, then Clay. Locke was clearly out of his element, running distance, and Clay appeared spent. His right thigh was wrapped with an elastic bandage, and he was limping noticeably.

I wonder if my limp is that obvious, Cody wondered. *If it is, Clay's gonna come after me, no matter how bad he's hurtin'. He's one tough dude. And speaking of tough, I wonder where Cabrera is. I know he didn't start ahead of me, but he can't be far behind, even if he did belly flop in the water jump during the last event. And I know he went four and one in basketball, same as me. Man, if he sees me like this, it'll be like a shark smelling blood.*

Cody hit two miles in 12:18, wincing at the pain—and slowed his pace. His wounded gait was enough to carry him by two giant competitors, barely shuffling along in the early afternoon heat.

On a short, steep hill, he struggled past Pierce Boy, who was coughing and sputtering like an old lawn mower.

A quarter mile later, the course took Cody through a park. He saw Chop standing near a sign that said KEEP DOGS ON LEASH. "You're in first, little brother," his friend bellowed, hopping up and down as if he were standing on a hot griddle. "It's all you, homey! You're gonna win this thing!"

"I'm in first?" Cody gasped. "You sure?"

"That's for reals, Code! This thing is yours. Now, go get it!"

I hope I can get it, Cody thought. *But if this pain*

gets any worse, somebody's gonna have to come and get me! In an ambulance.

He pressed on, looking down to make sure someone hadn't actually driven a railroad spike into his ankle—because that's what it felt like now. *Okay*, he told himself, *only about three-quarters of a mile to go now. I can endure anything for that long, can't I? But my ankle is killing me! This is so frustrating that I feel like I'm gonna grind my teeth down to powder.*

He almost groaned out loud as he came to a slight grade and began shuffling his way up. He could barely flex the ankle, and found himself getting almost no push off. He had to fight the reflex to wince with every other step. Halfway up the one hundred-yard incline, he swiveled his head over his left shoulder and risked a look behind him.

The second-place runner was so far behind that he looked like a kid's action figure. He was too far away to identify at the moment, but Cody could tell he was closing the distance between them.

He looked skyward. *I don't understand, Lord*, he prayed. *I worked so hard getting ready for this competition. I never thought I would actually have a shot at winning the whole thing, but here I am, ready to win. And I feel like I've earned it. Then this happens. If there are better all-around athletes here, I can live with them beatin' me. But I don't want to lose because of a stupid injury! Please make the pain go away. Please help me be able to run, instead of hobbling along like I'm doing now. Amen.*

Cody turned his head for another glance backward. Whoever was chasing him was only about 150 yards behind now. Still not close enough to identify, but definitely close enough to be a serious threat to the Ultimate Athlete title.

Whoever that is, he thought glumly, *he's gonna blow by me like I'm a telephone pole, unless this pain and stiffness go away. There's no other way I can win.*

He tried to shorten his stride even more, but the pain persisted. He tried lengthening his stride. That made the pain spike to an almost blinding intensity. He thought he heard the labored breathing of his pursuer. *Can't look behind*, he warned himself. *That will show whoever's chasing me that I'm worried. And maybe he'll be able to see in my face how much I'm hurtin'.*

Soon he could hear the soft, scraping footfalls clearly. Whoever was chasing him down was a good runner. *This guy runs almost as quietly as Drew*, Cody noted.

Ten seconds later, Cody realized he had been wrong. The chaser didn't run *almost* as quietly as Drew; he ran exactly like Drew. Because it was Drew.

"You're really favoring that left ankle," Drew observed, his voice clear and strong, despite the streams of sweat trickling down his forehead.

"It's pretty bad," Cody answered grimly.

"You think you should stop, have it checked out?"

"No chance, man. It's not swelling or anything, and it's not getting worse as I run."

Of course, Cody admitted secretly, *it hurts so bad that I don't know how it could get much worse.*

"I don't know, Code. I think you should shut it down. You don't want to do permanent damage."

Cody felt his jaw clenching. "Like I said, Phelps. No way. I've busted a gut for two whole days. I've worked too doggoned hard to get where I am. Look, I can see that I'm slowing you down, so just get your speed on and take the gold medal. I can still get second. Which is way better than I ever dreamed."

Drew ran stride for stride with Cody, his eyes focused forward. "How much farther to the finish?" he asked.

Cody managed a weak laugh. "Dude, you're way better at figuring stuff like that than I am."

Drew nodded and looked at his chronograph. "I've been running for about fourteen minutes, so we're about three minutes away, maybe more if we don't pick up the pace."

Cody stared at his friend in disbelief. "You wanna pick up the pace? Be my guest. I'm just trying to survive here."

Drew nodded again. "Okay. Just stay steady. But if the ankle starts getting worse, you gotta stop. Promise me that."

Cody wagged his head furiously. "I'm not promising anything. Except that I'm never gonna do something like this again. Now, take off."

Instantly, Drew accelerated. Cody marveled at how quickly Drew's quick, efficient strides put distance between the two of them. He risked a look over his shoulder. Someone else was in sight, little more than a dot against the horizon, but there was still a lot of ground ahead. That dot would have plenty of time to grow into a full-blown threat to his silver medal.

Cody's heart lifted a bit as he saw the 2.5-mile aid station about one hundred yards ahead—which was about the same distance between him and his new pursuer.

Cody drew closer to a table filled with paper cups of water and yellow green sports drink and blinked as he saw someone standing near the aid-station table, extending a paper cup to him. "Phelps?" he asked incredulously.

Drew smiled, handed him the cup, then began jogging beside him.

"Only about a half mile to go, Martin," he said casually.

"Yeah. A half mile of excruciating pain. You didn't have to wait for me, you know. You're gonna mess up your time."

Drew narrowed his eyes. "I wasn't waiting for you, Cody. I'm done."

Cody heard himself groan. "Flash ... don't do this. I don't want you to. You deserve to win. You earned it."

"I'm not doing anything for you, Cody. I am spent. Really. I just wanted to see how many guys I could pass before I burnt myself out. It was fun pickin' guys off, but I killed myself to do it. Hit the first mile under five minutes."

Cody's eyes widened. "Really? That is smokin'!"

Drew shrugged. "Then I made it to the two-mile mark in 10:48."

"You shoulda run a more even pace."

"Nah. It woulda ruined my pick-off game. Listen, Code, I'm not being gracious here. I am *gassed*. Both calves are on the verge of cramping up. It feels like rottweilers have chomped on to each one. And they haven't bitten down really hard yet, but it could happen anytime."

Cody dabbed at his forehead with the sweatband he wore between his wrist and elbow. "Are you for real?"

"Everything I have said is true. Now, if you're sure you're gonna finish this thing, bum ankle and all, then you might as well finish strong. Cabrera's only about seventy-five yards back now."

Cody sighed heavily. "Aw, no! Cabrera?!"

"Don't worry about him. Worry about you. Quit waddling and start running!"

"Yes, sir," Cody said sarcastically. "But what about you?"

"I'm gonna jog for a while. Cool down. Try to finish in the top five or so. But you never know, I might get a second wind and change my mind about things. So you better start putting space between you and me."

Cody nodded solemnly and tried to pick up his pace. He was sure he could sense Drew slowing and shortening his strides, trying to boost the always precarious Cody Martin confidence.

Presently, he felt his ankle starting to numb, ever so slightly. It still felt weak and stiff, but the edge had been shaved off the agony. He wheeled 180 degrees, running backward for a while, to give his ankle a change of pace—and to study Cabrera's progress. He didn't care what Cabrera might think. If he was closer than one hundred yards, the race was over anyway. He figured there was a little more than a quarter mile of course ahead of him. Cabrera was a strong distance runner, specializing in the 3200 meters. A seventy-five-yard lead was nothing to him.

About seventy yards now, and counting—or more accurately, subtracting! Cody surmised a few moments later. *Hmm, he looks like he's laboring a bit though. His head is kinda doin' what the cheerleaders say— lean to the left, lean to the right. And it looks like his fists are clenched. He's pressing. He's not running relaxed. Of course, neither am I—*

With about four hundred yards left in the race, Cody found himself walking. *Huh,* he said to himself. *I don't remember deciding to walk. What's up with me?*

He started to run again and almost collapsed from the pain. "Oh, yeah," he mumbled. "*That's* what's up."

He tilted his head to the sky. *Please, Father God,* he prayed. *Strength. Just the strength to go about four hundred yards more. Four football fields.*

He tried to run again, more gingerly this time. The pain still lurked, chiseling its way deeper into his ankle, but at least the joint didn't feel as if it would buckle. He heard three sharp, barking coughs behind him and whipped his head around.

Cabrera was ten yards back and closing steadily. Cody expected his opponent to accelerate and blow by him in a discouraging burst of speed. Instead, he drew near, then matched the ungainly Cody Martin, Wounded Runner, rhythm.

"That ankle must be bad," Cabrera observed, his voice empty of any compassion. "You're limping."

Cody found himself having to set his jaw to avoid bursting into tears. "Yeah," he panted, trying to sound brave, "it's messed up. I'm just trying to finish."

"I finally got you," Cabrera said. "I'm gonna beat you. This will be payback for the football upset in eighth grade. For showing me up in basketball, too, getting me yanked out of a game. Remember that? And one more thing—I can't believe you made varsity in football this past season. You're not better than me. Oh, yeah, and as far as track this year, you guys beat us in the four by 800 at districts, but those other guys carried you. You should have given your medal to me. You know I can beat you in the open 800. Anyway, see you at the finish line—*if* you make it to the finish line. And that's a pretty big if. You look like you're about to cry."

If only you knew, Cody thought. "Just go ahead and win," he said. "But, just so you'll know, I will make it to the finish line, even if I have to crawl."

"Whatever," Cabrera yawned. Then he lowered his head and charged forward.

Cody strained his eyes. He could see the large white banner that signified the finish line, looming about one hundred yards ahead. He swiveled his head around for one last look. Clay and Drew were dueling about seventy-five yards back.

If I can just keep moving forward, Cody assured himself, *they won't catch me. C'mon, Martin, just a 100 meters left. You eat hundreds for breakfast. Time to kick it in.*

Cody almost laughed as he tried to unleash his kick—which turned out to be a just slightly faster limp. Ahead of him, Cabrera appeared to be slowing down, probably feeling the fatigue of two days of competition.

With seventy yards to go, Cody wrinkled his forehead. *Whoa*, he thought, *Cabrera looks like he's running into the world's strongest headwind. The dude's almost standing still!*

Cody realized he would catch Cabrera if his rival didn't speed up. Of course, he would, though, when he heard Cody moving up on him. He would look behind, panic, then sprint like a madman and break the tape.

Oh well, Cody thought. *Might as well throw one last scare into Cabrera. Just for old time's sake.* He willed himself to hobble a little faster. Fifty yards from the finish line, Cody and Cabrera were running stride for stride. Cabrera hadn't panicked when Cody chased him down. He hadn't even looked surprised.

"Look," Cabrera said, seeming to be concentrating on matching Cody's pace, "I want to whip you, Martin, but not like this. It's not a fair fight. So, we finish together, deal?"

Cody had heard the world "surreal" used a lot. He had even uttered it a few times himself, especially when trying to impress Robyn in freshman English. But he hadn't truly grasped the word's essence. Until now. "Deal," he said, warily.

As the duo closed in on the finish line, Cody suddenly became aware of applause like crashing waves, along with exhortations of "Finish strong!"

He pumped his arms, straining against pain and fatigue. He could feel himself wincing with each stride, but he didn't care anymore. Cabrera was with him like a shadow. The ex-Nugget cheerleader and a redhead who could have been her evil twin held a finish-line banner peppered with the logos of sponsoring companies.

"It's a tie! It's a tie!" Cody heard Cabrera yelling at an official at the finish line, as he and his archrival lunged for the banner.

Cody scooted to his left, making room for Cabrera on the top of the three-level awards stand. He nodded, coaxing Cabrera to bow forward and accept his gold medal first. The ex-cheerleader carefully draped the medal around the athlete's short, thick neck, then gave him a peck on the cheek.

Cody smiled as Cabrera straightened himself and tried to look tough as cameras clicked all around him.

As I live and breathe, Cody observed, *I do believe Bobby Cabrera is actually blushing.*

Cody dipped his head to accept his gold medal, but he pulled back before the ex-cheerleader could get her candy-apple lips on him. The dodge drew laughter from the onlookers.

"Hey, you two, shake hands," called a photographer with a camera setup as big as the TV in Cody's bedroom. Cody half-turned to Cabrera and extended his hand. Cabrera hesitated a moment, looking at Cody's hand like it was a dead fish.

Finally, reluctantly, he accepted the handshake. Cabrera's grip was cold and reptilian, and he felt his rival squeezing hard, no doubt trying to make him wince.

Cody squeezed back. He could tell Cabrera was fighting a wince of his own. "Just because I let you tie me," Cabrera said through a forced smile, "don't think I am getting soft. This coming season, I'm gonna be in your face every sport. No mercy."

"Bring it on," Cody said.

Cody hopped down from the award stand and went to congratulate Clay on his silver medal and Phelps on his surprising bronze. "Hey, Martin," Cabrera called behind him.

Cody turned. "Yeah?"

"Come with me for a second. And, by the way, I want you to know that I respect your game and all. But like I said, the next time we face off, it's gonna be on again. Now, come on."

Cody frowned but followed Cabrera obediently into the crowd.

Cabrera stopped in front of a small, gaunt woman, who looked to be in her early thirties. "Mama," he said in an uncharacteristically soft voice, "this is the guy who loaned me his bike pump. You still got it, right?"

The woman smiled and dipped her hand into a purse the size of his dad's briefcase. "Of course, Roberto." She handed the pump to her son, who passed it on to Cody. "What you did was very honorable, young man," she said. "Helping a fellow competitor—you don't see sportsmanship like that anymore."

Cody shrugged. "It was just the right thing to do. And just so you know, ma'am, Bobby—er, I mean, Roberto is the real gold-medal winner. He showed a lot of sportsmanship by letting me finish with him. I was injured, and he could have finished me off, but he didn't."

Mrs. Cabrera enveloped her son in a hug. Bobby blushed and wriggled free. "Mama!" he scolded through clenched teeth, but Cody could tell his heart wasn't in the rebuke.

"Anyway," Cody said, stepping backward, "I have to go find my guys. Big ups on the gold medal, dude. And, nice to meet you, Mrs. Cabrera."

Mrs. Cabrera smiled. "*Vaya con Dios*, son."

"That's the only way to go," Cody said, as he turned and limp-jogged away.

Cody rode home with Doug and Pork Chop. When they arrived in the Martin driveway, Cody slid out of the front seat and accepted rough hugs, first from Doug, then his "little" brother, who now had to be 230 solid pounds, only ten pounds behind his older sibling.

Then he stood, facing Chop, who closed his eyes for nearly a full minute before speaking. "Well, Code, we did the good-bye thing already a few days ago. I don't have another one in me."

"I don't think I do either, Chop. But I do want to say thanks for coming up and supporting me." He fished his gold medal out of his sweatpants' pocket. I wouldn't have this hardware if not for you. And, uh, I'd like you to have it."

Chop took a step backward, holding a palm toward Cody. "Uh-uh, dawg. You worked too doggoned hard for that thing. All that runnin' on a bum wheel—that was like, whoa! There's no way you should give that gold away."

"But, Chop, I want to give it to you. Something to help remember me by, you know?"

Chop smiled warmly. "What I'll remember, little brother, is the years of friendship. And what I'll remember is you standing here, ready to give up your gold for me." He tapped a thick forefinger against his head. "I don't need a medal to help me remember all that. It's all right up here. I can play it, like a DVD, anytime I need it."

Cody nodded and exchanged a final fist-pound with his best friend. "Vaya con Dios, Chop," he said quietly.

"That's Spanish, right?"

"Yeah. It's good advice in any language."

"I'll see what I can do to follow it. You know, what you said about you and me and heaven—I can't get that out of my head. It's stuck there, like gum."

Cody chuckled softly. "Good." Then he turned away before Chop could see the tears spilling from his eyes.

Chapter 7
Whoa, Baby!

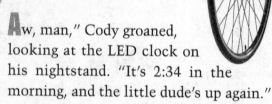

Aw, man," Cody groaned, looking at the LED clock on his nightstand. "It's 2:34 in the morning, and the little dude's up again."

He rolled onto his back and listened to the insistent "A-waaa! A-waaa! A-waaaaas" coming from the nursery, across the hall from his bedroom. He waited a moment, expecting to hear the soft padding of Beth's feet or the heavy thuds of his dad's footfalls in the hallway. But the only sound continued to be the increasingly urgent crying of week-old Porter James Martin.

"Aw, for Pete's sake," he grumbled, swinging his legs out of his bed.

"Wassup, little dude?" he asked, leaning over Porter's crib moments later. "You hungry again?"

Carefully, he lifted Porter from the crib and cradled him to his chest. "You're about the size of a football," he told his brother, "only a whole lot softer."

He tiptoed down the stairs and into the kitchen. He plucked a bottle from the refrigerator and placed it in the microwave. Removing the bottle forty-eight seconds later, he tilted it and squeezed two drops of its contents onto the back of his hand, being careful not to baptize Porter in the process.

"Okay," he said, "nice and warm."

He held the bottle to Porter's lips, and the baby took to it like Pork Chop to a chocolate milk shake. He moved to the living room and sat in his dad's recliner, watching Porter go to work on the bottle.

Presently, he looked up to see his dad and Beth standing at the foot of the stairs, smiling at him. "Go back to bed," he whispered. "Get some rest. I got this."

"You sure?" Beth yawned. "I mean, you have a game tomorrow."

Cody wagged his head. "It's a late-afternoon home game. I can sleep all morning if I need to. Now, both of you, scoot. Me and the little dude need some brother time."

Cody waited for Porter to finish the contents of his bottle. Then, remembering Beth's instructions, he lifted the baby to his shoulder and gently patted his back.

The resulting belch made him laugh out loud. "That was impressive, for an eight-pounder! That one woulda made your Uncle Chop proud."

Cody stood and began pacing the living room, speaking to his brother in soft, soothing tones.

"Where do I begin?" he said. "There's so much to teach you. See, little PJ, there's this recessed metal handle on some basketball courts, the kind of courts that can be removed from a gym when it's time for other sports or activities. Anyway, these thingies are smack-dab in the center of the free throw lines. So, if you use them as little landmarks, you'll always be dead-on centered for your free throws. That's important, 'cuz the key to free throws is shooting 'em all the same. It's all about form and repetition and concentration.

"Oh, yeah, and remember this, too—if you're inbounding the ball from the end of the court, step out, to the side, before the ref hands you the ball. See, you don't want to get caught directly behind the backboard on an inbounds play; if you do, you're likely to have the ball ricochet right back at ya.

"And we're gonna have to talk about track, too. About running even splits. About when to throw in a surge. About accelerating through the turns to psyche out the guys trailing you. See, if you can put some distance between you and them in the turns, when you hit the straightaways, it'll demoralize them, because the distance seems farther on a straight plane. Anyway, I think that's about enough for tonight; it feels like you're asleep, and I don't want to risk wakin' you up by yammering on.

"But, the bottom line is that I'm gonna teach you all about sports—and all about life. It won't be long before I can start reading Bible stories to you. Jonah, Samson, Joseph, and David—he's one of my favorites. Speaking of favorites, wait till you meet your Uncle Chop. He nearly busted a gut when I called him and told him you were named for him. He said, 'Give little Porter a big hug from me—but a big, *gentle* hug. Don't you go hurtin' my boy!'

"Dude, I miss Chop so much. But you know, you have helped ease the pain. Just like Chop's friendship, Drew's friendship, and all the people at the church helped ease the pain back when Mom died. God has always taken care of me, and I know he's gonna always take care of you too. And I know, I just know, that I'm part of God's plan for watching over you, PJ. So remember, no matter what happens, I got your back, my little brother."

Cody stepped carefully up the stairs and gently placed Porter back in his crib. He covered him up with a blanket festooned with multicolored rocking horses, then stood back, watching Porter fidget for a moment, then relax and settle into a deep sleep.

He turned and glided toward the doorway, pausing at the threshold to utter his new favorite prayer, the one that had replaced "Help!"

"Thank you, Father God," he whispered, tilting his head toward the sky. "Thank you, thank you, thank you."

Epilogue:
The Pork
Chop
Email

Hey, Chop,

Sorry it's taken me a while to answer your last email. Things have been crazy busy. That is so cool that you're starting on the varsity O-line at your new school. Way to rock, big brother!

Hey, you asked about a LOT of Grant people in your email. Here's an update for ya:

Brett and Bart Evans: Brett's still the better athlete of the two. He's a good two steps quicker than Bart in the forty. But, dude, Bart's arm is a rocket launcher. He's seeing a lot of action at QB, and he's throwing beautiful tight spirals that are a pleasure to catch.

Terry Alston: Believe it or not, he's starting to show me something, maturity-wise. He's out for football, and for the most part, he's keeping his head level and his mouth shut. He told me to say, "Tell Chop he's still the man. And I wish he was here. Tell him to move back by the time we're seniors so we can take state in everything!"

ATV and Brendan Clark: Word is, they're both seeing a lot of action at Eastern Colorado. In the season opener, Clark intercepted a pass and took it fifty-eight yards to the house. And I heard that while practicing kickoffs, ATV booted an old ball so hard that it exploded! Now, that could just be an urban legend or something, but if it's not true, I don't wanna know!

Craig Ward: He's my homey in the defensive backfield. He calls the two of us the SDC's—for shutdown corners. I can't shadow wideouts the way he does yet—especially 'cuz my ankle is still a little tender—but I'm working hard to hold up my end. And get this—two weeks ago against Holy Family, Ward snags this weak sideline pass and returns it for a TD. Then he gets to the end zone and dunks the ball over the goalpost crossbar! Is that sick or what? The guy's just a shade over six feet and he gets that kind of air with his football gear on? I can't wait till basketball season. The first time Alston sets him up for an oop, the crowd is gonna go nuts!

Robyn Hart: She's not wearing glasses anymore. She got contacts. I kinda miss the glasses, but there is something about those brown eyes. Beth calls 'em cocoa eyes. Dad calls her "a lovely young woman." If you could see her, you'd call her a "fly honey." Anyway, she was dating this junior for a couple of weeks, but that's over now. How do I feel about that? You'll have to guess. But I will tell you one thing. I had a pretty good game against HF, and afterward Dylan's smacking me on the shoulder pads, saying, "That's my white boy!" —just like you used to say. Anyway, Robyn comes up and smiles that sorta crooked smile of hers and says, "Funny—that's what I call him too." Make of that what you will—and wipe that smirk off your face will ya? I can feel you smirking all the way from Tennessee.

By the way, I know you and Robyn had your issues. I know she got in your face every time she thought you were acting like a stereotypical jock knucklehead. But she cares about you. She wrote something for you. Hang on, I'm gonna cut and paste it in:

Wind and Cloud

I am the cloud
You are the wind
You can push me away
When I try to befriend
I enjoy the soft breeze
On days you are calm
But you can be cold,
Doing less good, more harm.
I try to get close
You blow me away
When all else fails
I just drift . . . and pray
So often together

We go hand in hand
Will we always be close
Like the sea and the sand?
Sometimes I feel helpless
When I must drift where you will
Then watch as you leave me
While I must stay still
You move me along
When I'm stuck—it's true
And often I wish
That I could move you.
But how can a cloud
Give aid to the wind?
All I have to offer
Is to just be your friend.

So, there you go, big dawg. You've inspired poetry.

Terrance Dylan: Speaking of TD, he's a hoss! He's six feet, two inches now, and a solid 170 pounds. He's diesel. He's playing linebacker, and some of the old-timers in the bleachers are saying he's gonna be the next Brendan Clark.

Drew Phelps: He got in his thousand miles over the summer, and he's tearing it up in cross-country. He broke seventeen minutes for the 5K in the first race of the season, and he's pretty much a man among boys out there. I don't think anybody's gonna threaten him until districts—or maybe when they go up to a big meet in Denver. By the way, he says to tell you he prays for you every day. That makes two of us, at least.

Dad and Beth: They've showed up for every game, with Porter wrapped up like a mummy, even though it's not cold yet. Dad even showed up for the intrasquad game. He smiles all the time now. I haven't seen him smile as much since before Mom got sick. I think he's truly happy for the first time in a long time. If you could see him rolling on the floor with Porter and all these stuffed animals, I know what you'd say. You'd say, "Dawg, your pops is like a fat baby with lots of cookies." (Now, if only I could get Dad to stop calling me "Buddy-o" in front of the team . . .)

As for Beth, she calls me "Dude" all the time, which is kinda cool, I guess. She sure knows what she's doing when it comes to Porter. You know how Coach Clayton said Drew is a natural runner? I think Beth is a natural mom. Speaking of which, I heard her making a dentist appointment for me a couple days ago, and she introduced herself as "Cody's mom." It used to hurt me when she said that, but this time it didn't. I'm not saying it felt good or even comfortable. But it didn't hurt. So, who knows . . .

Coach Clayton: The first day of school, he comes bouncing up to me in these tired old Adidas and says, "For the love of Henry Rono, dawg, you sure you won't run cross-country for me this fall? I gotta wait all dadgum year—till track season— to coach my dawg?" I have to say, I did think for a while about running cross-country. Running is in my blood, but so is football. The first time I walked by the training room and saw

Dutch tightening face masks and pumping air into helmets, I felt like throwing on some gear and goin' to tackle somebody. Preferably Bobby Cabrera.

Goddard and Gannon: Goddard is still a little bit of a porker, and Gannon still talks a better game than he actually plays. But they are the studs of the JV team. Goddard is playing left guard, taking on guys twice his size and not backing down one inch. Gannon says he's finally acquired a taste for vegetarian cuisine, but I caught him chowing down on a double cheeseburger in the back booth at the Double D. He tried to tell me it was a tofu burger, but there's nothing like that on the menu. Anyway, he's playing wide receiver, and he's got a pretty good handle.

Porter James Martin: You've seen the PDFs I've sent, so you know that Porter is the coolest little dude ever. I can't tell you how much it means to me that Beth and Dad let me name him after you. I can't wait to see the two of you together. I'm already telling him all about his Uncle Chop. I don't know if any of it is sinking in, since he's only a month old, but you never know. Anyway, the boy shares your name, so make him proud.

Tanner DiMarco: I know what you're thinking: Who in the wide world of sports is Tanner DiMarco? Well, he's this new freshman. Built like a stick figure. I think he might have some developmental challenges, but I'm not exactly sure what they are yet. Anyway, during the first week of school, some guys start making fun of him—you know, Schutte, Neale, and that crew. So, I head over toward them, thinking I'm gonna have to crack their heads together or something. I'm praying for wisdom, courage, strength—the whole package—and something comes over me. I get to Tanner and I high-five him. He's wearing these old black Chuck Taylor high-tops, so I compliment him on 'em. He smiles. Then Robyn appears at my side. She goes me one better—she *high-tens* the dude, then gives him a hug. You know Robyn.

"What's this?" Schutte snorts, "Be Kind to Retards Week?"

I know what you're thinking right now, Chop, but I didn't rock him. I just stared him and Neale down, Clint Eastwood old-school style. I told him, "If I hear that word again, it's gonna be Thump a Couple of Punks Week!" Schutte takes a step toward me, but it's a tentative step. "Don't," I say. Next thing I know, Ward is at my side. "Thump a Coupla Punks Week?" he says, all excited. "I want a piece of that!"

"Me too," Dylan says, from the other side of me. He folds his hands in front of him and says, "That's my favorite week of the year!"

Needless to say, Schutte and Neale slink away while the slinking is good. But that's not the best part of the story. The best part is that now, whenever Tanner DiMarco walks through the halls, everybody is fiving him, giving him dap. Ward always bellows, "Tan-NER!"

Anyway, you oughta see Tanner's eyes. It's like someone has switched a light on inside his head. When I see what's happening, I think about what Mom always used to say, about how people are God's hands and feet. And I think about Greta Hopkins. Remember her? And I hope that, wherever she's going to school these days, some people are reaching out to her the way we're trying to do for Tanner.

Whoa, dude, this is like the longest email I've ever written. I gotta bounce, but one thing before I go. . .

A lot has changed between you and me in the past year, and change is hard. But the good news is that nothing changes when it comes to you and God. You've moved farther away from me but not farther away from him. I'm still praying for you every day. Blake said he emailed you about a cool church near you. I hope you've checked out the youth program there—so, have you? If not, don't wait, big man. Get yourself there. And, as you might guess, I'm gonna keep checking. So save yourself the harassment from me.

And, just to give you a little more incentive, if you keep putting this off, you're gonna find a bunch of Tennesseans for Jesus on your porch, eager to haul your booty to church. So don't resist, Chop. Resistance is futile.

Feel this, big man. God loves you like crazy. He misses those times when you were in Sunday school every week, sitting next to me and explaining to all the other grade-schoolers why Peter was "the dopest disciple of them all!" God misses the way he was front-and-center in your life. I miss that too.

Remember this summer when you asked me what I would wish for if I had only one wish, and I said I'd wish that you didn't have to move. Well, I answered you too quickly. My number-one wish, for real, would be that you'd FINALLY open that door in your heart and let Jesus *all* the way in. Don't keep opening the door a crack, making him stand on your porch while you talk to him for a few minutes, then close the door in his face again. It hurts when you do that. Dude, there are about eight bazillion angels ready to rap their brains out when you get on God's team. And my mom will be leadin' them. C'mon, big brother, get your faith on.

Your best friend,
Cody Martin

P.S. Get your faith on (in case you forgot).

Acknowledgments

Big, shiny MVP awards to the following people:

Bruce, Robin, Kristen, and everyone at Zonderkidz for believing in this series.

The Mill Valley High School football, track, and basketball teams for reminding this has-been jock how the games are played in the twenty-first century.

My YMCA league teams—the Super Saiyans, the Legends, the Vikings, and the Dragons—for the privilege of coaching you and for the many lessons you have taught me about sportsmanship and courage.

Barbara Scott for your strong early support of Cody and his story. There wouldn't be a book, and certainly not a whole series, if not for you.

Toby Mac for penning the foreword to this series. You captured "The Spirit of the Game" perfectly.

Jami Hafer for the poem "Wind and Cloud."

Dave Dravecky for the athletic expertise and the spiritual wisdom you have shared with me, through conversation and the fine books you have written.

Tim Hanson for being my teammate and, more important, my friend through so many seasons of sports and of life. Even though we weren't able to coauthor this series, as I had hoped, your mark is on every book. And every life that this series touches, every accomplishment it inspires, I share with you.

Chapter 1

A Death in the Family

As Cody lay on the field, his mind drifted back to the day of his mom's funeral.

Cody squirmed in the front pew of Crossroads Community Church, trying to wriggle his way into a comfortable position. He sighed heavily and twisted around to study the scene behind him. He felt dozens of eyes lock on him, then nervously dart away. Except for those of Mrs. Adams, his grade school Sunday school teacher, who gazed at him lovingly. She was five rows back, but Cody could see that her eyes were red and puffy from crying. He tried to smile at her and then turned around. He usually sat in the back of church—the very back, in one of the metal folding chairs lined against the rear wall of the sanctuary.

"The best seats in the house," Cody always called them. They allowed him to slip out to the restroom or the foyer without disapproving stares from his mom and dad—or that busybody Mrs. Underwood. And, during the occasional Sunday when he couldn't follow Pastor Taylor's sermon, he could pass the time by counting bald spots, then figuring the percentage of follically-impaired men in the congregation. The last time he counted, 23 percent of the Crossroads men were Missing Hair Club candidates.

The percentage was slightly higher if you counted Mr. Sanders, whose sandy toupee always rested atop his head at a jaunty angle, like a dozing badger.

On the rare Sundays when Pork Chop accompanied Cody to church, the duo would slip out to the foyer during the special music—which usually wasn't very special at Crossroads—and feast on the remaining donuts on the refreshment table.

The good donuts, the ones filled with jelly or crowned with multi-colored sprinkles, were always gone, plucked by those devoted enough to come to the early service. But the remainder, the glazed ones with watery icing beading on them like perspiration, were better than nothing.

A Death in the Family

"Donuts—at church!?" Chop said once while sucking glaze off his fingers with loud smacks. "Now that's a heavenly idea! It's almost worth coming to church every Sunday. Almost."

Cody leaned forward and rested his elbows on his knees. Pork Chop was in church again today, but there would be no joking. Chop sat three rows behind Cody, sporting a too tight suit and sandwiched between his father and his mammoth half brother, Doug.

Cody had begged his dad to let Pork Chop sit by him, but had been informed that such an arrangement wasn't "proper funeral protocol."

Cody was bookended by his dad and Gram Martin, his paternal grandmother. Cody looked at Gram, who looked older, plumper, and sadder than the last time he saw her, even though it was just two weeks ago. She was sniffling quietly and dabbing at her eyes with a tattered lavender tissue. It was no secret that Cody's mom and Gram Martin didn't get along, but the grief seemed genuine.

Or maybe it's regret, Cody thought. Maybe Gram is thinking of all the shouting matches she and Mom got into and feeling guilty.

He turned his attention from his grandmother to the coffin at the front of the church, just below the pulpit.

I can't believe my mom's in there, *he thought, shaking his head. But it was true. He saw her in there only twelve hours ago. He had waited patiently in the foyer, pawing at the carpet with his foot as he listened to the choir practice "Amazing Grace," which was his mom's favorite hymn during the final weeks of her life. The choir sounded somber, but pretty good—better than he had heard in a long time.*

When the singing stopped, Ben Woods, of Woods Family Funeral Home, approached Cody. "You can see her now, if you wish," Ben said, with a calmness and compassion that Cody guessed had taken years to perfect.

Wish. The word floated through his mind. I wish this whole thing wasn't real, he thought. I wish I were anywhere but here. I wish Mom weren't lying dead in a giant box.

Cody felt Ben's fingers touch his elbow. "Would you like me to get your father, Cody, so you can go in together? He's in the pastor's office."

"No," Cody said, surprised at how hard it was to make a sound. "I kinda need to do this alone."

Ben nodded and led Cody to the front of the sanctuary. With practiced ease, he raised the top portion of a two-piece lid and locked it into position.

A Death in the Family

"I will give you as long as you need," he said. "I'll close the sanctuary door behind me when I exit, to give you some privacy. Just come and find me when you're ready. And, Cody, I am very sorry for your loss."

Cody felt his head nodding. He had waited until he heard the door latch click before he allowed himself to look at her.

They had done her hair. Wispy honey-colored bangs rested on her forehead, the ends nearly touching her thin eyebrows. Cody noted the thick makeup layered on her face, like frosting on a cake. It reminded him of the makeup the high school thespians wore for their spring musicals.

He heard himself exhale sadly. When she was alive, Linda Martin rarely wore makeup. She used to joke that she wanted people to see a few lines on her face. "Maybe then they'll let me teach adult Sunday school—not just work the nursery," she would say.

Cody's dad had a different take. "You don't need makeup, Lin," he told her regularly. "Why cover up perfection?"

But the folks at Woods Family Funeral Home had covered up plenty. Cody remembered relatives talking about funerals from time to time. He recalled snippets like, "He looked so natural," and "She looked so peaceful lying there in the coffin."

But his mom didn't look natural or at peace. She looked empty. He studied her face. Slowly, tentatively, he raised his left hand. It floated toward her, as if under a power not his own.

He let his fingertips rest for a moment on her cheek. The skin felt cool, lifeless. More like rubber than human flesh. He drew his hand back.

I hope I forget how that felt, *he thought.* That's not how I want to remember things.

"Bye, Mom," he whispered. "And thank you. Thank you for everything you did. The meals—the laundry—the help with homework. Coming to my games. I wish I had been more grateful. I'll try to say something about you tomorrow, but I'm not sure I can. If I can't, I hope you'll understand. And I hope that, somehow, you know that I'll always love you. Please, God, let there be some way for her to know that—and to know how much I miss her already."

He felt his throat tighten. He turned toward the exit, gazing at the stained glass windows as he walked down the rust-colored carpet that ran down the center of the sanctuary. The last window depicted a sunrise scene, with a white dove gliding across the morning sky. Inscribed above a golden rising sun were the words, I AM THE RESURRECTION AND THE LIFE.

A Death in the Family

Before he opened the door leading to the foyer, Cody let his eyes move from the words to the church's high ceiling. "Yeah," he whispered solemnly, hopefully. "The life."

Cody felt himself being led to the sideline, Brett Evans under his left arm, Pork Chop under his right. Both were five foot eight, two inches taller than he was, so his feet glided across the short-cropped grass as they left the field. It felt almost like walking on air. He looked into the stands and saw about half the home crowd standing, rendering a polite smattering of applause. He searched for his dad's face, but knew he wouldn't find it.

This is gonna be just like seventh grade ball, he thought. *He's gonna keep blowing off games 'til the season's over. Only now I won't have Mom in the stands. I could always count on her. Now I don't have anybody.*

Pork Chop helped Cody lower himself to the bench. "It was Tucker who ear-holed you, right, Code?" he asked.

"Either him or a Mack truck."

"Well, just watch what happens next. It's gonna be payback time next time we're on defense. I'm gonna hit him so hard that it'll knock the taste out of his mouth."

"Chop—"

"Don't argue with me, my brother. Just chill and watch the fun. We're losing by twenty anyway. I gotta do something to keep myself motivated."

Cody started to protest and then shrugged his shoulders, which brought the stabbing pain back again.

Coach Smith kept him out of the game's final four minutes, during which Clay scored again on the QB sweep. On that play, Pork Chop chased down Tucker from behind and rode him to the ground, even though it was obvious that he was a blocker, not the ball carrier. After the referee raised both hands to the sky, signaling the TD, Chop smacked his palms against the sides of his helmet, feigning anger at himself for being duped. Then he extended a thick forearm to Tucker and jerked him to his feet.

Tucker stood, wobbly and disoriented. It reminded Cody of the newborn scene in *Bambi*. The fullback got off the field just in time to avoid Central's receiving an offside penalty on the ensuing kickoff.

By the Monday morning following the Central game, the pain in Cody's neck had faded. The pain in his heart, however, still burned. He smiled anyway.

He smiled at Coach Smith, who saw him in the hallway at school and asked, "You doin' okay, Code?"

He smiled at Robyn Hart, his friend since fourth grade, when she told him, "Good game on Saturday."

And he smiled at Kris Knight, the new student that Principal Prentiss introduced him to in the school office before first hour.

This is weird, Cody thought. *You don't even have to be happy to smile. Just like you don't have to be mean to play football. You just have to act like it, and I guess no one knows the difference.*

"Mr. Knight," Mr. Prentiss was saying, "welcome to the eighth grade at Grant Middle School. This is Cody Martin. This is his second year as one of our orientation mentors. He will be accompanying you to most of your classes, as your schedules are almost identical. He will help you find your classrooms, the cafeteria, and whatnot."

"Yeah," Cody said, injecting artificial happiness into his voice, "we have great whatnot here at Grant."

Mr. Prentiss unleashed a laugh that was as fake as Mr. Sanders's toupee.

As they headed toward first-period PE, Cody tried to think of a conversation starter. "So," he said finally to his "mentee," as Mr. Prentiss called them, "you do any sports back at your old school?"

Knight had arms like broomsticks, and Cody noticed that his feet splayed out at 45-degree angles when he walked. It was as if his left foot and right foot disagreed on which direction their owner should be going. Still, you had to ask. Polite conversation—that's what Dad and Mr. Prentiss called it.

Knight cleared his throat. "Nah, I'm not really into sports. I mean, I like them and everything, but I have asthma. I played in the pep band, though. Clarinet."

Cody nodded. "That's cool." He saw Knight looking at his white football jersey, which bore a faded blue number 7. John Elway's number.

Cody heard the throat clear again. It sounded like a dirt bike engine revving. "You must play, huh, Cody?"

"Yeah, I can't remember a time when I wasn't playing something. T-ball. Y-league hoops. Pop Warner football. Age-group track meets. You name it."

"That's cool," Knight said, unconvincingly.

They entered the gym and sat together on the first row of wooden bleachers. Ten boys, divided into shirts and skins, were playing full-court basketball. Another seven or eight sat on the bleachers near Cody and Knight, awaiting their turn.

Coach Smith, who taught PE in addition to coaching football and wrestling, paced the sideline, wearing a pained expression on his face.

"Come on, ladies," he chided, his voice weary and sandpaper-rough from the past weekend's game, "this is physical education. So let's get physical. Sewing class is third hour. Porter, if Alston beats your entire team down the court for one more uncontested layup, you knuckleheads are doing push-ups until your arms fall off!"

"Who's Porter?" Knight whispered loudly. "Is he that big dude?"

"Yeah," Cody said with a laugh, "the one who's sweatin' so much he looks like he's been dipped in baby oil. That's Pork Chop."

"Pork Chop?"

"Yeah. See, when he was a baby and cutting teeth, his dad used to give him pork chop bones to gnaw on. Drove his mom crazy, from what I've heard. Anyway, that's where the nickname comes from. His real name's Deke."

"That's his real name? What's it short for?"

"It's short for nothing. Just Deke."

Knight nodded. "What should I call him?"

"Well, Chop always says, 'Call me anything—just don't call me late for dinner!'"

Knight laughed politely.

Cody leaned back, resting his elbows on the second tier of bleachers. "I probably should tell you one thing about Chop," he said. "You probably notice that he's got quite a tan."

Knight nodded again.

"Well, his dad's white. His mom was black. Still is, I guess. She bounced a couple years ago. See, we don't have a lot of, uh, African-Americans in this part of Colorado. It was hard for Chop's mom. It's been hard for him too. I've been with him when people have driven by and called him—well, you know. You should see his eyes when it happens. I mean, he's a tough guy, but when people say stuff like that, racial stuff—"

"People still do that? In Colorado?"

"People still do that. And worse. Anyway, he can be a bit sensitive about the subject. Just so you know. But don't get the wrong idea. He's cool. He has a great sense of humor. Funniest guy in the school, as far as I'm concerned."

"So, you guys are friends?"

"Best friends." Cody felt his voice cracking as he said the words. He hoped Kris Knight didn't notice.

They turned their attention back to the game. They watched Pork Chop grab a rebound, swinging his elbows viciously from side to side as two opposing players tried to steal the ball from him. "Get offa me!" he snarled.

"Watch the 'bows, Chop," Coach Smith snapped.

"Wow," Knight said. "I wouldn't want Pork Chop mad at me."

Cody whistled through his teeth. "No," he said, "you sure wouldn't."

After one of Pork Chop's teammates shot an air ball from the free throw line, the shirts team gained control of the ball and launched a fast break. Their point guard drove down the middle of the court, stopped abruptly at the top of the key, and lofted a jump shot that slid through the net without even grazing the rim.

"Wow," Knight said, "who's that guy? He's good!"

Cody watched Terry Alston stand and admire his shot for a moment, then turn and lope downcourt with smooth, easy strides.

"That's Alston," he said. "Best athlete in the whole school. Just ask him. He transferred here from a private school in the Springs—Colorado Springs. He says basketball's his best sport. And, from what I've seen in gym class so far, he's probably right. We should be pretty good this year. We'll have a new coach. It should be fun."

Cody stopped talking. Knight had been nodding politely, like a bobble-head doll, but it was obvious he wasn't that interested in what kind of year the Grant basketball team would have.

Gotta shut up, Cody scolded himself, *before you bore this poor guy into a coma.*

He focused on the game again. Alston intercepted a lazy crosscourt pass and then dashed downcourt, sandy hair flying behind him. It looked like another easy layup for the shirts team.

Cody was startled when a huge blur streaked by. He thought he heard a cheerful "Check this!" as Pork Chop passed in front of him.

Alston slowed slightly as he zeroed in on the basket, sizing up a right-handed layup. As he released the ball, Pork Chop accelerated behind him. With a loud grunt, Chop propelled his 190 pounds into the air and extended his left arm.

He got just enough of his fingertips on the ball to direct it off the bottom of the backboard.

"Yeah! That's what I'm talkin' about!" Pork Chop's chest-deep bellow echoed off the gym walls. "How do you like that, TA? How do you like the taste of leather in the mornin'?"

Alston shot a glare at his much larger opponent. He retrieved the ball and then fired a hard chest pass at Pork Chop's stomach, but Chop caught the ball deftly and set it gently, almost lovingly, on the baseline.

"It's your ball, Hollywood," Chop said. "I swatted your mess outta there, remember?"

A Death in the Family

Cody could feel the tension building like the heat in a sauna. Pork Chop and Alston had been trash-talking since summer baseball. Now they stood only a few feet apart, staring each other down. Pork Chop's thick arms were folded across his chest, while Alston's hung at his sides, his hands clenching and unclenching.

When Coach Smith stepped between them, Cody felt a long exhale escape from his chest.

"You best save your aggression for the gridiron, Porter," Coach said evenly. "Besides, your team's down by four buckets. Not really a good time to be yappin'."

Alston went into his trademark sneer. "Yeah, Port—"

"And you," Coach Smith cut in, "don't even start with me, Blondie. You know, if you would have gone out for football, you two could have settled your differences on the field. But no, I guess some of us are just too pretty to play football, aren't we?"

Goal-Line Stand
Written by Todd Hafer
Softcover 0-310-70669-6

In *Goal-Line Stand*, Cody's football coach decides to move him into the wide receiver position, forcing Cody to compete with his good friend Brett Evans for a starting spot on the team.

Full-Court Press
Written by Todd Hafer
Softcover 0-310-70668-8

In *Full-Court Press*, Cody tries out for the 8th grade basketball team. He makes the team, but his temper and upbringing to "turn the other cheek" are tested when he's challenged to a fight.

Second Wind
Written by Todd Hafer
Softcover 0-310-70670-X

In *Second Wind*, Cody becomes a solid distance runner and builds a friendship with Cole Phelps, the team's reclusive distance ace, who teaches him a lot about running and life.

Stealing Home
Written by Todd Hafer
Softcover 0-310-70671-8

In *Stealing Home*, Cody is injured playing baseball in the summer league and learns some hard lessons about the fine line between courage and foolhardiness.

zonder**kidz**

Three-Point Play

Written by Todd Hafer
Softcover 0-310-70795-1

Cody struggles with jealousy when his teammates Pork Chop Porter and Terry Alston are called up to the junior varsity and varsity teams, and Cody is thrust into a leadership role on the freshman basketball team.

Cody's Varsity Rush

Written by Todd Hafer
Softcover 0-310-70794-3

As Cody moves into a public high school dominated by vocal non-Christians who challenge his beliefs, he finds himself reluctant to speak up in defense of his faith—or even to admit he is a Christian.

Author Todd Hafer brings you more sports action with Spirit of the Game sports fiction!

Coming November 2005

zonder**kidz**

zonder**kidz**.

We want to hear from you. Please send your comments
about this book to us in care of zreview@zondervan.com. Thank you.

Grand Rapids, MI 49530
www.zonderkidz.com